SWORD OF THE WILDERNESS

YOUNG AMERICA BOOK CLUB · EDUCATION CENTER · COLUMBUS 16, OHIO

By Elizabeth Coatsworth

*The words of the song were very simple, but the melody was full
of tenderness and a sense of something coming.*

YOUNG AMERICA BOOK CLUB

A division of Weekly Reader Children's Book Club

PRESENTS

SWORD OF THE WILDERNESS

By Elizabeth Coatsworth

ILLUSTRATED BY

HARVE STEIN

THE MACMILLAN COMPANY

NEW YORK

Young America Book Club Edition

PRINTED IN THE UNITED STATES OF AMERICA
BY AMERICAN BOOK-STRATFORD PRESS, INC., N. Y.

To Aunt Nelly and Uncle George Chester
and Uncle Frank Reid

this book is dedicated with love and a deep
gratitude for the many days spent under
their roofs, and the many stories with
which they filled our childhood.

"We got our bread with the price of our lives, because of the sword of the wilderness."

CONTENTS

CONTENTS

SWORD OF THE WILDERNESS

I

THE GARRISON HOUSE

EARLY on a fine August morning of 1689 Seth woke in his attic bed to the sound of Ensign's barking.

"Indians!" he thought, and then immediately, "Is everything shut tight?"

He had a mind that saw things quickly and completely in images. As he pulled on his clothes a small picture flashed before his eyes of his father closing each of the shutters the evening before. Had he, perhaps, left one a little open? Seth did not think so. Then he saw the image of Zeke Hinton barring the doors. He, himself, had gone out later to look for the cow, but he had certainly put the bar in place when he came in.

The barking below continued in explosions of sound. He heard people moving and went to the small window that opened from his loft and peered out. Below him in the early morning light the fields of cropped hay and of standing corn shone with a sparkle of dew that made them almost as bright as the water of the little harbor beyond. There was smoke coming from the Snows' chimney next door, rising up straight and undisturbed by any wind. Mr. Snow was standing in his doorway stretching his arms. A young cockerel was raggedly crowing; nothing stirred in the woods; not even a crow flew across the sky.

Only Ensign continued barking, breaking the tranquil hush of the early morning. Then as Seth still stared anxiously and intently toward the edge of the woods beyond the rail fences, his eye was caught by a slight movement in the grass below him. It was the Snows' gray cat with the white face stepping through the shorn hay on wet paws, and Ensign gave a final roaring bark as the cat slid out of sight.

"All that row over a cat!" thought Seth, half angry, half relieved. He closed the shutter and barred it, and went downstairs whistling. "Be still, Ensign! You old fool!" he exclaimed, cuffing the hound's ears. "Father, it was that gray cat of the Snows going by. You'd think every tawny between here and Quebec was in the woods to hear him. But there isn't a thing stirring and Mr. Snow's up and out and there are three crows feeding in the stubble near the edge of the woods."

"We're not at war," said Samuel Hubbard slowly. "There hasn't been any trouble for nigh ten months or more."

"Yes," said Zeke Hinton in his quick high voice, "but it's nearly fall now, and there's not an Indian come into the village to trade for a fortnight. I feel trouble near, like a cold wind in my bones."

Everyone knew that the Hintons were a nervous pair. He had come to Pemaquoit as a carpenter. He was not a real settler in his blood. Even baby Zeke cried all day as though he drank fear in with his mother's milk. Ten days ago they had left their own place to come into the Hubbards' garrison house. Seth knew that his father had thought it unnecessary at the time although he had said nothing; and of course he had not refused them shelter, since they asked for it.

Now while his mother quietly put away the bullet molds that she had brought out, and pushed back the lead from the hastily kindled fire, Mrs. Hinton still sat huddled on the settle rocking the baby in her arms and moaning. Seth's young sister Abigail raised the lid of the pot on the crane, and a heartening odor of bean porridge and steaming pork came into the room.

Mr. Hubbard opened the door, his gun still on his arm, and looked about. The early sunlight fell across the threshold, full of simplicity and peace. After a moment he stood his gun against the wall, but Seth could see that he still was listening and watching intently.

Abigail trotted out of the pantry with a pitcher in her hand.

"There's no milk, ma'am," she said to her mother.

"No, you remember Jenny broke through the fence yesterday," her mother answered quickly.

"She always goes to the alder swamp," said Seth. "I'll take the pail down and milk her."

His mother's hand went to her mouth in a quick uncertain gesture. She started to speak but checked herself, looking at her husband. Seth was fourteen now, strong and well grown. In these times it was not for women to try to make the decisions; it was enough for them to trust to their men's courage and judgment. If the whole household was to stand shivering every time an old hound barked, they should never have come here to the edge of the wilderness at all.

So when Samuel Hubbard had taken a last searching look once more from the open door and then nodded to Seth, she only said, "Take Ensign," and spoke sharply to Abigail.

"Drat the child!" she thought to herself as she stirred the porridge. "Why must she bring in the pitcher just now?"

A small path, worn by Seth's own feet, curved from

4

the door down through the fields toward the woods.
Seth started out boldly enough. He could still hear his
father speaking to his mother; behind him the sea gulls
were crying and the tide made its unceasing lisp against
the rocks along the shore; to his left lay the little harbor where he so often went swimming, and the fishing
sloops at their anchors faced into the rising tide near
the Barbican. The cold dew that beaded the cobwebs
spilled across his bare feet, delicious and fresh. All
these things Seth scarcely noticed, but he was very
aware that Ensign was not following him; that Mr.
Snow was splitting wood behind his barn; and that the
crows were still strutting about in the lower field, the
early sun whitening their glossy plumage and casting
long shadows on the green stubble.

"They wouldn't be acting so bold if there was anyone about," Seth said to himself.

The fields sloped down to the woods and the alder
swamp in the corner. At his approach the crows flew
up. He could not see his house now, beyond the shoulder of the hill; but he heard the steady sound of Mr.
Snow's ax at the chopping block and a chickadee calling out in a friendly way from a tamarack. In the
swamp just beyond the fence rails he heard a muskrat
plump into the water from a log, and he thought he
heard Jenny, the cow, stirring in the bushes.

"Co' boss, co' boss, co' boss!" he called, clanking the pail in his hand a little. Everything was just as it always was when he went to find Jenny. The earth under his feet reassured him; the stillness and salt smell of the air, even the twirling and twisting of a single hanging leaf when nothing else moved, these were peaceful things far removed from danger and terror.

Seth had a sudden complete lightening of the heart. His tense muscles relaxed and he sighed unconsciously. They weren't at war any more. Most of the soldiers had gone back to Boston months ago. Only old women and the two Hintons still talked about Indians.

In a corner of the field there was a large anthill of piled sand and chaff, and before going into the thicket after Jenny Seth walked toward it to see if the ants had finished cleaning the raccoon skull he had put on it a few days before. As he was standing engrossed he became aware of long shadows, cast from behind him, moving swiftly over the grass toward his own.

The Indians had come.

II

The Alarm

SETH had not the slightest chance to escape and knew it. He wheeled away from the shadows to face his captors. The savages were naked except for loin cloths and moccasins, their faces were painted vermilion, and now he caught the smell of bear's grease. He knew one of them, even through the paint—Bedagi, Big Thunder, who had sometimes traded with his father. The others were strangers. He could see several more Indians beyond them beginning to move toward the Snows' house.

7

His captors trussed him hurriedly with thongs while Bedagi questioned him.

"How many in house?" asked Bedagi, and all their eyes were fixed on his, unwinking as snakes' eyes.

"Father and Zeke Hinton and four of the fishermen from New Inlet," said Seth readily.

"You lie!" said Bedagi, striking him across the mouth.

Seth spat blood. "Go and see and I hope they shoot you, Bedagi," he said. He was not afraid now, but angry and thinking fast.

The men moved up the slope, leaving him with Bedagi and another Indian out of sight in the hollow. There had not been a sound. Beyond lay the houses with their doors open; and Seth thought of Abigail setting out the wooden bowls for breakfast and Mrs. Snow with her new baby. Only one thing could warn them.

Seth gave a loud war whoop. One of the Indians with him swung up his tomahawk, but Bedagi struck it aside.

"Mine," he said, nodding at Seth.

The first Indian left them without a word and began running after the others who had given up their attempt at concealment and were racing toward the houses, yelling like fiends. From where he stood, Seth could see Mr. Snow run out from behind the barn, his ax still in his hand, and dodge toward shelter.

An Indian stopped, leveled his matchlock, and fired. Mr. Snow stumbled, fell, rose again, and walked slowly forward, his hands to his side. Seth watched an Indian overtake him and strike him down with his hatchet. From his own home he heard the hound barking and the sound of shots. Were his family being butchered in the dooryard, or had his father got the great door shut? The shots went on, now two or three shots, and then two or three more as the guns were reloaded and re-primed. It wasn't butchery, it was attack; the garrison house had been built strong for defense, his father had a chance. He clenched his hands—if he were only there to help! His mother would be loading his father's gun, he knew, brushing the light hair back from her eyes. Even little Abigail would be helping with the bullets, but the Hintons would be only making a confusion. Perhaps Ezekiel would fire a few shots.

Hatchets were striking on wood, at the Snows'. Mrs. Snow had got the door shut then, but their house was not a garrison house. Even with men in it, it wouldn't be able to make much of a defense; and with Mr Snow dead, in a minute or two the door would be splintered through under their axes.

Bedagi fastened another thong about Seth's neck and twisted it over his brown sinuous wrist.

He pointed toward the Snows', and they, too, began

9

walking up the slope. The sea gulls were making a clamor, circling and screaming in the air.

They passed near Mr. Snow lying in a heap on the ground, already stripped and scalped. Only yesterday this had been a man who laughed at Zeke Hinton. "I'm moving in, too, when I get my baby's cradle made," he had said with a wink. Seth had never before seen a man scalped, and the sight made him feel sick. He stumbled as he walked and the thong about his neck jerked. Now he could see his own house. The Indians were making an uproar, whooping and howling. Whenever one dodged out of shelter to fire, Seth heard his father's matchlock roar from inside. One of the savages seemed dead, another was bleeding at the shoulder, though with the vermilion smeared on their chests it was hard to tell which was blood and which was paint. At the Snows' door, two men were chopping with their tomahawks. Already the oak planks had been cut through, and a man might easily have put in his hand to draw back the bar inside; but there was too much chance that a frenzied woman would strike at it with a knife or ax. There was plenty of time. Smash, splinter, went the axes, and the men working chanted in a sort of fierce rhythm.

Seth saw an Indian creep close to the side of the garrison house from the back. The man knelt, quiet and intent, over a pile of dry leaves and scraped pith which he had brought with him, striking his flint and then cupping the small flame between his hands. Two feathers were fastened in his scalp lock, and the early light shone along his oiled body and the fringed buckskin leggings that he wore.

"Smoke um out like bears," said Bedagi, grinning.

At that moment the wrecked door beside them gave way, and the Indians, hooting and shrilling, poured in. Yanked by his cord, Seth followed Bedagi. Like a drowning man, he had a last glimpse of his own house, dark and large against the glitter of the bay, the smoke rising peacefully from the chimney and a line of more sinister smoke curling up its side as the kneeling Indian crawled away to safety.

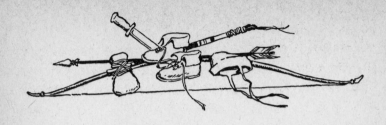

III

THE SETTLE

MRS. SNOW sat on the settle by the fire, one arm about four-year-old Persis, the other hand over the child's eyes. Her lips were white and she was singing, a hymn Seth thought. There was no sign of the baby. An Indian seized Persis and pulled her out of Mrs. Snow's arms. The child shrieked.

"Oh, don't kill her, don't kill her!" cried Mrs. Snow in a low voice, trying to control her terror.

Seth lunged forward in spite of his choking collar, throwing his bound body against the arm of the Indian who held the child.

"I'll carry her!" he said. "I'm strong. Sell her at Quebec." He leaned against the Indian, looking up with his gray eyes into the man's black eyes. "She'll be worth a new gun, anyhow," he said, repeating slowly, "I'll carry her."

The child was screaming. The man dropped her to the floor. He made a motion, as though stopping her mouth, a motion as though cutting her throat. Seth understood. He must quiet Persis or her master would kill her anyway. If she could be silenced, he might save her.

"Persis," he said, "I'll tell you a story—this is only a dream, Persis. Persis—"

He turned to Bedagi. "Let my arms go free," he said. "I can't get away."

Bedagi untied the buckskin about his wrists, but the thong was still tight at his throat. Seth took Persis in his arms and turned with her toward the window.

"See the gulls, Persis," he said quietly. "What a big white one that is!" He went on talking to the child soothingly, and her cries hushed to sobs, and she put her arms about his neck. "There's a bonfire, Persis," he said, his own mouth dry.

In the two minutes since he had entered the Snows', the fire against his own house had gained. In this dry weather the wall itself would soon be in flames. No help would come from the town, on whose outskirts they lay. The war whoops and the firing would have been plainly heard; but each garrison house would be preparing for its own defense and receiving its neighbors, and the handful of soldiers would never venture out until they knew how large a force had come against them. They could not look for help, and the fire was burning brightly. He did not know whether his family knew it or not.

But at that moment the back door opened, a small man shot out with two buckets in his hands, ran along the side of the house, splashed both buckets over the fire and ran back again and into the house before Seth knew for a certainty he had ever been there. Only one Indian recovered from his astonishment enough to fire at him and he apparently missed.

"Huzzah, huzzah for you, Zeke Hinton!" yelled Seth, beside himself.

Bedagi jerked him from the window. Seth scarcely cared what was done to him by now; but he knew that if he died Persis would die, too, and the weight of her in his arms filled him with a sense of responsibility.

Mrs. Snow still sat on the settle, but they had tied her arms and she had a rope about her neck, too. The Indians were looting the house. The air was filled with white feathers from the feather beds they had slit with their knives and were using now to stuff things in. Flour and ham and maple sugar, all went in together; clothes and shoes, bolts of linen and wool from Mrs. Snow's loom, blankets, spoons, a Bible, and a wooden doll in a red calico dress. In their search chairs were overturned, chest drawers pulled out with a crash, but through the noise Seth thought the firing and yelling were less frequent from outside. The Indians were in a hurry. They were only a small party and had already lost several of their men. They had no wish to be caught at their work by a rescue party of townsmen and soldiers.

Through the confusion Mrs. Snow's eyes caught Seth's in a long look. She was trying to tell him something, trying to make him understand and help her. She dropped her eyes a moment to the settle on which she was sitting and then looked again at him.

He dared not nod his head, but his expression showed her he understood. He went on talking to Persis and, when he could, he picked a piece of charred coal from the fire. He began to draw pictures for her on the smooth back of the settle and in and out of the pictures of horses and fish and cats he put letters, which no Indian would notice but which taken all together read:

"Look for baby under settle."

IV

Carried Away

A HOOT like an owl's sounded. The Indians hastily assembled their loot; a pack was given to Mrs. Snow and
one to Seth, which he carried on his back, still holding
Persis in his arms. The Indians, too, had each a load,
which they carried on their backs from a strap across
their foreheads, bringing the weight on their necks.
Seth and Mrs. Snow were both in a fever to be gone.
Seth guessed that when the attack had begun the baby
had just been fed and, being so very young, had fallen
asleep and not wakened in spite of all the noise. Mrs.
Snow had used the few minutes' delay at the door to

dress herself and hide all signs of the baby's existence, but even now one cry would send a savage back to dash out the little life against the doorpost. He was in a fever of impatience as Bedagi picked up a mug of beer from the trestle table which had been filled less than an hour ago for Mr. Snow and, drinking it, set it again in its place, wiping his mouth with the back of his hand.

Now at last they were out of doors. But a small apple tree grew near the front door, and the Indians paused a moment while several picked the ripening apples and one Indian brought some brands from the hearth and threw them against the splintered door. The savages had withdrawn from Seth's house—one carried a dead comrade across his shoulders, and Seth saw that another was indeed wounded. As they began their march, he, coming near the rear, reached out and kicked the brands apart as he passed by. The blow from Bedagi almost threw him to his knees, but no one took time to rebuild the fire he had scattered. He judged the house would be saved unless his father waited too long before daring to unbar their door.

One more look he gave toward his home that he was leaving perhaps forever. Now that the Indians were gone it looked empty and peaceful, with its closed shutters and its small rising wisp of smoke. Even at that distance he could see the marks of bullets in the wood, and a crow, no longer disturbed, came cawing up from the swamp to spy out what had taken place. Two hollyhocks stood unbroken in late bloom by the door.

As he turned away, his head ringing with Bedagi's blow, a movement about the house attracted his attention. The shutter in the upper window of his own loft room was cautiously drawn back, and for an instant a white handkerchief fluttered and then was gone. It was his mother waving farewell to Seth, promising to do all that might be done for his redemption, saying goodbye to her only son as he was carried away into captivity.

V

THE MAGICIAN

THE leader of the war party was named Natanis, a tall
man with a scar across his cheek. He was older than the
others and spoke with an air of authority, and his
orders were immediately obeyed. His eyes, in the
vermilion and black of his face, looked out calm and
watchful, neither cruel nor kind, and his mouth re-
minded Seth of the mouth of a cat, set in a sort of sculp-
tured smile. He led the way at a swift even pace which
Mrs. Snow, just up from a sick bed, and Seth, with his

load and the child in his arms, found hard to follow. "Canoe byme bye," said Bedagi behind him, and Seth set his teeth and kept on. Persis clung to him, her eye- lashes wet with tears and her face streaked with them. If he dropped back or slowed down, it would be she who would first pay the price. A little way in the woods, two more Indians joined them, bringing the number of their party up to ten or twelve men. These two had evidently found Jenny and butchered her, for they carried heavy loads of meat on their backs.

Seth saw immediately that Natanis knew the country like the palm of his brown hand—it was likely that he had lived and hunted here before the white settlement had been made. He led the way toward the swamp that almost cut Pemaquoit into an island, then followed a small stream through the spruce woods, wading in the shallow water. As Seth walked he tried to turn stones under his feet so that they might appear displaced and show the way they had gone to anyone who might fol- low, but a sharp jerk from Bedagi brought him to a halt.

"I not kill you three four times already," he said fiercely. "Now kill you quick, you do one thing more."

That Bedagi had shown great forbearance toward him he knew well, and now he dared take no further risk for Persis' sake. He stumbled on, wondering if he could ever fulfill his promise to carry her to Canada. He had had no breakfast, and the blows he had received made him feel dizzy, so that he walked like a sleep walker.

She wriggled in his arms. "Seth," she said, "let me down."

They were now following a game trail south and she trotted along in front of him intent on keeping her place in the line. In her own young mind she understood what had happened and she understood, too, that she must be brave. When they stopped once to rest, she pointed to the belt of one of the Indians where something hung.

"Father's," she whispered to Seth, her lips trembling.

Soon he found his breath and carried her again. He knew they were going down the peninsula toward the open sea. The smell of salt was strong in the air and the sun was in their faces. He heard the gun at the fort. Boom! boom! boom! it went. It was probably to announce that the attack was over and gather the men for council. Possibly some of their neighbors might try to rescue them, but that would be dangerous both for the rescuers and captives. Hurrying on, with Persis in his arms, he hoped that no one would follow.

Now, Natanis was leading the way more slowly. The

Indians as well as their captives were heavily laden, and they were out of danger of immediate pursuit. At one point Natanis halted and, taking two round loaves of bread from one of the packs, divided it among the party. Mrs. Snow sat down and leaned against a tree. She refused her share of bread. "I baked it yesterday for my husband, Seth," she said. "I haven't the heart to eat it, now."

"Eat for Persis' sake," said the boy.

Her eyes blazed suddenly in her white face. "Seth, that is his scalp," she answered and said nothing more. Persis ran to her, and she held the child, soothing her, her gaze fixed on nothingness.

When her master ordered her to her feet she rose and picked up her bundle, but her eyes looked through him as though he were not there.

Bedagi encouraged Seth. "Soon come boats," he said. "Not far now."

After the food and rest, Seth felt stronger, and his head was clearer. He saw that the Indian in the rear was covering the trail behind them, brushing out any marks of feet, smoothing disturbed branches. Sometime toward the middle of the afternoon they came upon three canoes at the edge of a cove, pulled up under the trees and hidden beneath branches and moss.

Here there was a great deal of talk among the Indians, some apparently urging a stop for the night and some anxious to take the boats and press on. Finally, the oldest of the party built a small fire and sat down beside it, opening as he did so a pouch that hung at his side. The other Indians left him and scattered into the underbrush, but as he followed Bedagi, Seth saw the old man take out dyed feathers, tobacco, and the shoulder blade of some wild animal, which he placed before him.

In about half an hour the old man called and the savages returned. They listened intently to what he told them and then they all began to laugh. Bedagi turned to Seth in high good humor.

"He make magic," he explained. "Bone get warm. He see picture on bone of men who come after us. Only one man. We catch him sure." His eyes twinkled maliciously.

The baggage was hidden in the underbrush, and the three prisoners were taken by their masters to a spot about a third of a mile away from the fire, while the rest arranged an ambush for the one pursuer. They all seemed to trust the magician completely.

"But, Bedagi, maybe twenty men come," said Seth hopefully. "Maybe you all be killed."

"Bone he say one man," said Bedagi. "Never lie, that wildcat bone."

While they waited, Mrs. Snow took her knitting from

the pocket of her apron and began working on a half-finished stocking. Her dress was torn in several places by briars, but she had straightened her hair and looked wildly domestic, seated on a log, with a naked savage beside her, his tomahawk in his hand.

"I've got to do something besides think, else I shall go mad," she said. "Persis, let us say 'The Lord is my Shepherd' together."

The Indians sat in silence, full of their own thoughts. Before the psalm had reached "through the valley of the shadow of death, I will fear no evil," a shot rang out from the camping place, followed by an infernal clamor.

The two Indians listened intently.

"They got um," said Bedagi.

VI

Burial by the Shore

THE camp, however, was not in any state of rejoicing. A prisoner was, indeed, bound to a tree; but before his capture he had managed to kill one more Indian—as it happened, the man who had Mr. Snow's scalp in his belt. This was a young savage who had often come to Pemaquoit to trade, and the English called him Captain Job. Now he lay beside the other man who had been killed in the attack on the garrison house.

All afternoon the Indians busied themselves making deep graves which they lined with birch bark cut from near-by trees in long sheets. They blacked their faces with gunpowder, and then, chanting and lamenting, buried the two warriors in a seated position facing the East. With each man they put an ax, two pairs of moccasins, a kettleful of beef, and a heavy belt of wampum. Then, opening the feather-bed covers in which their loot was stored, they chose a few objects to put with their dead: with the man killed in the attack, two frilled shirts and a china teacup; with Captain Job, a broadcloth coat that had once been Mr. Snow's and a pair of his shoes with silver buckles, which would have been much too small for the Indian ever to have worn in life. They hesitated about their guns. But these were too precious. Several of the men had only bows and arrows and hatchets for hunting and war. Natanis shook his head, birch bark was laid across the open graves, then logs, more bark, and lastly earth, covered once more with moss and pine needles so that no stranger could have told that the earth had ever been disturbed. That evening, though the rest of the Indians and the prisoners ate, two of the closest friends of the dead men sat upon their graves all night, fasting and keeping vigil.

Seth several times tried to come close enough to the English prisoner to see who he was, but Bedagi forbade it. The man was left bound to the tree all night, but Seth and Mrs. Snow were staked out along the ground, each hand and foot fastened to a sapling by a thong;

and over Seth Bedagi laid a cover of small branches which extended beyond his body several feet on each side. And on these branches on one side lay Bedagi and on the other another Indian, so that he could not make the slightest movement without awakening them. But in spite of the discomfort of his position and the terror that lay behind him and the danger ahead, Seth was so wearied out that he slept all night long as though he were lying in his own bed under the eaves.

VII

Up the Coast

Mrs. Snow leaned from the canoe in which she sat with Persis, and spoke to Seth in the second boat. "It is John Hammond, and the baby is safe with your family," she said. "None of the others would follow us, but he hoped to find where we were encamped and to bring the soldiers during the night."

Her master struck her with his paddle. She was silent, and Seth saw her draw out her needles. She had raveled out the old sock and was beginning a new one, small, he thought, for Persis. The early morning light shone in her hair and along the ripples and made the pine needles gleam like glass. There was a delay on the shore, where three or four Indians stood about the tall burly form of John Hammond. They had unloosed his right hand and given him a piece of charred wood and a square of birch bark.

"Write," said Natanis. " 'Englishmen, you follow and Indians kill prisoners quick.' Put your name."

John Hammond was stretching his cramped hand.

"Give me time, Paint and Feathers," he said. "I'm not good at my spelling," and catching Seth's eye, he winked cheerfully.

Seth felt a warmth go through him. Alone with Mrs. Snow and Persis, all the responsibility of white manhood had seemed to rest with him. Now here was John Hammond with his shock of corn-colored hair and his eyes so bright in his brown face; John Hammond who went secretly fishing on Sundays and seldom attended meeting, who diced with the soldiers and laughed at the magistrates; John Hammond whom his mother used as a warning to him, "If you're not careful, you'll turn out no better than that ne'er-do-well." Here was John Hammond, himself, joking with the savages, insolent as a turkey cock and showing no more fear of them than a Mohawk. Unconsciously, Seth felt the lightening of a sort of race responsibility.

The message was written and fastened conspicuously to a tree near the fire. John Hammond was bound again, thrown into the third canoe, the cord about his neck fastened to one of the thwarts, and in silence the three canoes slipped along the shore with no sound but the slap of waves against their sides and the scream of the gulls.

All day they traveled northeastward along the coast. It was an almost windless day, so safe that the Indians did not follow the shore, but boldly paddled from point to point of land. The great islands of Monhegan and Matinicus lay far out to sea, and nearer them they passed smaller islands humped like whales; and the little waves breaking into spray on the windward sides seemed like the blowing of whales. The sky was mottled with clouds, but far to the east it lay luminous and clear.

"Over there is London," Seth thought. He had seldom been as far from the harbor as this, for his father was a landsman not fond of fishing. He felt taken out of his own troubles by the bright expanse of the ocean, with the land dropping away to the left, rimmed with hills like more blue waves, and the canoe rocking, and the necessity to shift weight carefully, balancing on all this expanse of water. Once the canoe Seth was in began to leak a little and he felt the cold salty water wetting his feet and clothing, but one of the Indians warmed some pitch they had with them and stuffed it into the leak. Another time, a seal raised its round head near by to watch them. It seemed to be counting their numbers as though to make a report of their passage, and then its smooth head was gone and Seth saw it no more.

But at last the heat of the sun which intermittently beat down upon them, and the dazzling of his eyes, and the salt smell of all the air that flowed over them, and the rocking of the canoe, and the steady motions of the naked lean back in front of him, made Seth fall asleep. Bedagi did not waken him, but he was roused with a start by the canoe's grating on a sandy shore. He rubbed his eyes with hands which had been left unbound. It was sunset and they had come to a beach in the shelter of a small cliff. Everyone jumped out and helped pull the canoes ashore and unload them, everyone except the wounded Indian and John Hammond who was still tightly bound.

While some were preparing a supper of hominy and beef before the fire, Bedagi took Seth with him to hunt white oak leaves for a poultice for the wounded man. There seemed to be a path up the cliff, and at the top Seth saw that he had not been mistaken. Before him lay what had once been an English field, plowed and planted to corn; to one side lay a blackened cellar hole and a chimney blackened but upright like a tombstone.

"There was a white man here," thought Seth, stum-

bling among the burrs and weeds. "Some day all Pemaquoit may be like this."

That evening the captives were given the worst of the
food, and John Hammond left the others and strode
over to where the warriors were feasting. Amid their
black and scowling looks, he thrust his hand into their
pot and, taking a hunk of the choicest meat, returned
with it to the others. A low sibilant sound of talk followed this exploit.

"They will kill you," whispered Mrs. Snow uneasily.

"They will, anyhow," replied John Hammond. "To
be certain of being killed is much like being certain of
being saved. It leaves one easy."

VIII

THE GANTLET

THREE days later they arrived at the Indian village on the Penobscot, from which the war party had set out. The Indians had repainted their faces for the occasion and insisted upon painting their prisoners too. Seth wrinkled his nose at the strong smell of bear's grease; he had a glimpse of Mrs. Snow in the next canoe looking like a witch in a fairy tale with Persis like a baby witch at her knee. Mrs. Snow was still knitting, faster than ever. It was a beautiful morning, and there was a spirit of excitement in the canoes. The men paddled fast, helped along by the incoming tide, racing one another; even the wounded Indian took a paddle and fell to work. The banks sped smoothly by, dark trees above a narrow tidewater line like a belt of white wampum between forest and river. Great herons rose at their approach from their fishing in the shallows, very slowly unfolding their long dark-bordered wings, slowly, slowly trailing their legs into the beautiful position of flight. An eagle in an oak on the shore, watching the fishing of the ospreys, flew across their path, and Seth saw the sun shine on his white proud head and the spread white tail.

The canoe in which Seth was sitting began to drop back from its position of leader. Seth, scarcely thinking what he was doing, seized an extra paddle and put his weight into the stroke. He heard Bedagi laugh behind him and their canoe crept up on its rival, slowly passed it, and again took the lead. Now the village appeared beyond the bend and the warriors gave their scalp yell as the boats tore forward, a yell for every scalp and every prisoner, answered from the village with more yells and the firing of guns.

The village lay a little back from the water, among

cleared land planted to corn. It consisted of a series of roughly parallel square houses made of scaffolding covered with strips of bark sewn together, with skins hung before the doorways. Many of the houses were still less elaborate, being only such wigwams as the Indians use in travel, but there seemed to be one building fifty or sixty feet long toward the center.

The whole town, old men, women, children, and barking dogs, were down at the edge of the water to greet the return of the war party. The prisoners were caught up into a great dancing circle and whirled about, amid chanting and stamping. Suddenly the circle opened and stretched out into a double line of young men and boys, who in some way had each managed to become armed with a stick.

"Run! Run!" the Indians cried to John Hammond and Seth. "Run, English! Run!"

With a terrible sinking of the heart Seth realized that he was facing the dreaded gantlet.

He glanced about on every side. The women were laughing; the children were jumping up and down with excitement, screeching; even the old men were convulsed with amusement; and the French trader whom Seth now noticed for the first time, standing on the outskirts, smoked his pipe and gave no answer to Seth's beseeching look.

It was John Hammond, a towering figure in a ragged shirt with his face a blaze of vermilion, who steadied him.

"I'll go first, Seth," he said in his matter-of-fact voice. "If you hear any little disturbance, run ahead while they're thinking about something else and dive into the first wigwam you see. Once inside you're safe."

Seth took a deep breath. He saw John Hammond's back bend as he dug his toes into the ground and started off. Seth followed close behind, moving as in a nightmare. He saw the first club fall on John Hammond's back and heard the whack of wood on flesh; then he saw Hammond whirl, yank the stick out of the Indian boy's hands, and begin to strike right and left, bellowing cheerfully, "Take that, you tawny you, and that! Seth, scoot, I tell you!"

And Seth scooted—a few blows fell on his back and his arms, raised to protect his head, but most of the boys were intent on the battle about John Hammond. Out of breath, in a great state of excitement but scarcely hurt at all, Seth ran into the first opening of a house that he came upon and sat down panting in its empty smoky dusk.

In a few minutes, John Hammond joined him, blood mixed with his vermilion paint, his clothes almost torn off him, but his club still in his hand, and a smile still on his face.

"I got a few good licks at those red satans," he remarked cheerfully. "Tarumkin, that squinting devil who was Captain Job's blood brother, wanted to have me killed for it, then and there, but the old men were tickled. They seemed to think that if thirty boys couldn't manage one man, they'd better take the consequences. Are you all right?"

"Thanks to you," said Seth. "You took the whole brunt."

"Just having a little fun," answered the big man looking embarrassed.

"Women don't run the gantlet, do they?" asked Seth.

"Not with these tribes," said John Hammond. "Their chances are good, if they can live through the winter. I think your chances are good, too. Bedagi likes you. Keep a straight back, but do as you're told, Seth."

He reached a wooden spoon into the pot that was steaming on the lodge fire and filled two bowls with broth, giving one to Seth and taking one himself. The hot fragrant liquid seemed to run into Seth's veins.

"But *you* don't do as you're told," Seth said, with admiration.

The man gave him a strange sad look. "Surely you

37

understand, Seth," he said soberly, "they will burn me for the Indian I killed. Then you must look out for the Snows. Forget about me. I'm a man and took my chances with my eyes open."

"Why did you ever come after us?" said Seth his voice sinking.

"I've known Mrs. Snow ever since she was no older than Persis," said John Hammond. He drank down his broth and wiped his mouth. "I would like a good drink of rum," he added cheerfully, but here are my friends coming and I bet Squint Eye is in the lead. Now you just recollect, Seth, there's no good wasting your breath begging favors off an Indian. It just pleases 'em to see you at it."

IX

IN THE COUNCIL LODGE

IT WAS to the council lodge in the middle of the village
that John Hammond was taken, his arms again bound
behind him, while the children threw dust and gravel
into his face. Seth was taken there, too, by Bedagi; but
no one paid any attention to him, and he knew that he
was involved only as a spectator in what was to follow.
But his heart was as heavy in him as though he had
been walking by John Hammond's side, his eyes smarting with the sand and his ears filled with the derisive
yells of his tormentors.

Once the leather curtains of the lodge had fallen,

however, all was decorum. The chiefs, old men and warriors, each sat quietly on his blanket in a circle about the outside of the room, and John Hammond stood bound to a post in the center. Natanis, who had led the war party, rose and gave a measured speech, toward the end motioning in the direction of the prisoner. When he had seated himself, Tarumkin, the squinter, rose and spoke passionately. Seth thought that a look of brooding and cruel pleasure came into the eyes of his listeners, and Bedagi leaned over to him to whisper with satisfaction, "Him say how kill Englishman."

Now an old man rose and spoke while all listened attentively.

"Him say," Bedagi translated, " 'Bring Captain Job's squaw. She say how kill um.' "

There was a murmur of approval about the circle. Tarumkin rose and said something with an evil grin.

"Squaws know how make last long," said Bedagi, whispering in Seth's ear.

"He sounds like a snake," thought Seth. "They're not men, they're snakes."

He would have given his life to save John Hammond. He watched a young man lift the curtain of the lodge door and go out. No one spoke. Each man sat gravely on his blanket, smoking his pipe, and the smoke rose into the quiet air. John Hammond stood at the post, awkward, large, grotesque in his rags and paint, never glancing at the Indians, his blue eyes fixed quietly on his own thoughts.

Seth was too tired to think. He saw only one thing to do and he must do it, though his flesh shrank from the thought of what would follow. Somehow, and soon, he must get near John Hammond, he must snatch up one of the tomahawks. He, himself, must kill him with one blow.

Then he would be in John Hammond's place.

The elkskin at the entrance was drawn back. Against the sunlight appeared two figures, and one was of a woman outlined on brilliant green and blue. The curtain fell again and in the dusk Seth saw that she was young, that her face was painted for mourning, and that she wore a cross about her neck. It was Captain Job's widow, come to determine what death John Hammond was to die.

Natanis rose. In a voice deep and musical he seemed to bewail the death of her husband, then his voice took on a sound like the sound of striking knives, and he turned and stared at the prisoner.

In a tense silence he sat down.

The Indian woman stood with her eyes looking at the ground, glancing neither at John Hammond nor at Natanis. After a few moments, she began to speak, hesi-

tatingly—almost like a child. Seth felt her listeners
stiffen with surprise and then the lodge seemed to grow
icy with disapproval. And still the woman spoke shyly,
scarcely above a whisper, and at last her voice trailed
off into silence. Tarumkin sprang to his feet, confront-
ing her fiercely; he poured out abuse upon her; his
voice, harsh and accusing, rang through the lodge; he
demanded something over and over again. But this
time the circle of Indians did not answer to his voice.
Their eyes were withdrawn. They were considering
within themselves.

When at last he had finished and was seated, the
woman again spoke. Her voice was full of the sound of
tears, of helplessness, of request. Soon she was silent.

No one spoke.

An old man rose. He went to John Hammond and
cut the thongs which bound him.

"You kill her husband," he said in broken English.
"She say what good to her we kill you? Who hunt for
her this winter? Who get meat for papoose? Who scare
off wolves? She say can dead man do this? She say can
burned man spear fish in spring? Now you belong to
squaw. You do what squaw say."

In two strides John Hammond walked over to the
woman and stood looking down.

"Mrs. Captain Job, or whatever they call you," he

42

said huskily, "you're going to have more meat this winter than anyone else in the tribe and the fattest papoose
going."

The same men who had meditated on the manner of
his death with such satisfaction a few minutes before
crowded about him now, slapping him on the shoulder,
laughing, thrusting their pipes into his hand for him to
smoke.

"Indians like him. Big chief some day," said Bedagi.

Like someone who has undergone all the weakness
and pain of a long sickness and then begins to con-
valesce, Seth followed Bedagi into the sunshine.

He felt hands clutching at his shirt. Mrs. Snow,
white beneath the paint still on her face, leaned against
him near to fainting.

"John Hammond?" her lips and eyes asked, almost
without sound.

The squaw who was with her, her new mistress,
pulled her away.

"He's sassy as a blue jay!" shouted Seth after her.

He had never before seen the sunlight so dazzlingly
bright.

X

THE DANCE

IN BEDAGI'S lodge, Seth found Bedagi's wife, his brother who had not gone out with the war party, and his wife and several children, none over seven years old, whom it took him some time to recognize separately and sort into families. The squaws were good to him. They gave him food and allowed him to wash the paint from his face, and one showed him a deerskin which he might have for his own and measured his feet for a pair of moccasins. They would have made him Indian leggings and a shirt, too, but he clung to his English clothes, soiled and torn though they were. Without understanding it exactly, he had a feeling that when he gave up the clothes he had worn at Pemaquoit he would cease to be the boy who had roamed the fields and woods there, and instinctively he tried to hold fast to his disappearing identity.

The thong about his neck had been taken off and a collar of wampum put in its place. That afternoon he went with the squaws and children gathering blackberries in birch-bark baskets at the edges of the clearings. The squirrels were very much interested and came to scold; they seemed to flow along the branches, which swayed under their weight. The little chipmunks sat on the near-by rocks, and Seth noticed again how the marking along their sleek sides imitated the striping about their eyes, so that they seemed to be staring with their whole bodies.

He was in a mood to enjoy all that he could of the moment in which he was living. After all, he thought to himself, his family was safe. Mrs. Snow's baby was safe, too, and John Hammond was now on the same footing as the rest. He earnestly thanked God for their preservation up to this point and picked blackberries busily with a grateful heart.

But Seth was mistaken in thinking that his immediate troubles were over. The next day another war party returned home with three men and a boy whom they had taken on the Sheepscot. He was away at the time of their arrival but learned later that they had run the gantlet and had bruised backs in consequence.

That night he heard sounds of singing and shouting from the great lodge, the measured beating of moccasins on hard earth, the thud of drums, and the dry throb of rattles keeping time, and found himself being led by Bedagi toward the spot. Bedagi only answered his questions with a grin. The place looked horrible to Seth, lighted by two fires in the middle and filled with almost naked savages, dancing, while their great shadows leaped along the walls. The men prisoners were all huddled in the center of the ring, between the fires and under a pole from which dangled several scalps. Just as Seth entered, an old woman threw a shovelful of hot coals straight in the chest of one of the men, who let out a sound, half oath and half shriek, at which the Indians burst into laughter.

From time to time a prisoner would be singled out, given a tomahawk, and ordered to dance about the ring singing the prisoner's song, while their captors joined them, dancing and mocking them. The men danced sullenly, their unwilling voices chanting, "I don't know where I go, I don't know where I go," for as none of them could speak the Indian language, Natanis told them the English of the song.

When Seth's turn came, he threw himself into the

motions, determined that if he must dance, he would
dance with a will. He leaped high into the air, then
stooped almost to the ground, and straightened again to
brandish his tomahawk, as he saw the Indians do,
thinking all the time of Squint Eye and of the pleasure
with which he would strike the tomahawk down on his
head, if only he dared. Compared with the Indians who
capered and danced with the agility and litheness of
wild animals, Seth was clumsy enough, but they ap-
plauded his efforts with approval. The play grew
rougher. Suddenly four braves rushed forward and
seized one of the men, each by a hand or foot, and holding him high in the air hurled him down on the ground.
Another ring surrounded Seth. He looked from face to
face and saw no look of pity in any of them. One put
his hat into his hands and they began throwing straws
into it, preparatory to some fierce game.

But what that game was to have been, Seth never
learned; for from the circle watching at the walls of
the great lodge an old woman and a girl of about his
own age detached themselves, carrying between them a
bag of hominy which they laid on the ground near
where he was standing. Then taking him by each hand,
they led him out of the circle. One of the most terrible
things about living with Indians, Seth had discovered,
was never being prepared for what was going to hap-

pen next. The faces of the squaw and of the girl were expressionless. He thought that they had bought him and were taking him outside to kill him.

"Bedagi," he called despairingly.

Bedagi appeared at his side, his eyes twinkling. He thrust his pipe into Seth's mouth.

"Squaw no hurt," he said benignly. "Squaw good to English boy."

The girl leaned over and patted Seth's hand, smiling at him, and there was nothing cruel in her smile. With a great sigh of relief, Seth allowed himself to be led outside.

He had been too perturbed on entering to notice the night, but now he saw that the moon had risen almost full and that the whole landscape seemed to lie in candlelight; only the shadow at his feet was clear and black. Most of the wigwams were empty, but in one he had a glimpse of John Hammond eating calmly by the fire, with an air of making himself very much at home. The old woman and the girl did not stop, however, at any of the lodges but passed along the edge of a cornfield and through some trees to a log house overlooking the river. They knocked at the door until a squaw, dressed like a white woman, but with moccasins on her feet, appeared and let them in. While the women and girl were talking and laughing, Seth looked about the

room. On the log walls there was a crucifix and a picture of a lady in a blue dress and mantle with a baby in
her arms, done on white doeskin, with a border of
painted leaves. The faces were brown, with something
of an Indian look, but it was pleasant to see anything
gentle after the violence he had just witnessed.

The squaw who had opened the door followed his
glance and smiled.

"Marie et Jésus," she murmured in French. "Notre
Dame des Bois."

"A Popish picture," he thought sternly to himself,
remembering his bringing up; nevertheless, he felt
safer and more at peace than he had felt at any time
since he had been captured.

There was a pile of skins in one corner of the room,
and Seth was sure that this was the French trader's
cabin and that the woman was the French trader's wife.
She went quietly about making them comfortable,
bringing them cakes of maple sugar and milk in the
usual wooden bowls, the first milk Seth had tasted since
the night poor Jenny had wandered once too often into
the swamp. At the first taste, an overwhelming feeling
of homesickness seized him by the throat. He could almost imagine himself at home on the stool by his own
fire, and he put down the bowl, unable to drink any
more for a little.

49

It was the trader's wife who by signs explained that soon the Indians would be drinking, then—she shrugged her shoulders—who knew? She smiled and pointed to Seth and the house. He was better here. Nothing would happen.

Soon the trader, having sold the Indians a keg of brandy for beaver skins, returned home, showing no surprise at finding strangers in his cabin. He spoke a little English.

"Your big frien', hé? Narrow thing they don' kill heem. Brave man, your frien'. I try to buy in morning, but Natanis no sell. Don' like to see them burn even you sacré English. The new prisoners? These Obenaki not so cruel like Iroquois. Just a leetle fun wit' them to-night. No harm."

It was the girl who asked him something which made the trader smile his white quick smile.

"That gal always, always make me sing," he said. "Sing that song about the trapper Cadreux with hees skeens coming down out of Ottawa. He heard Iroquois were at Calumet Isle portage—only chance hees Indian wife and friends had shoot the rapids in bateau. He go on trail and fire off gun to bring Iroquois away from river."

He shrugged his shoulders.

"Oh, yes, hees friends find heem later, dead in a little

grave he deeg for heemself before he die. Beside heem was poem he write on piece of birch bark with hees blood."

Without warning the Frenchman began to sing.

> *"Un de ces jours que, m'etant éloigné,*
> *En revenant, je vis une fumée.*
> *Je me suis dis: 'Ah, grand Dieu, qu'est ceci?*
> *Les Iroquois m'ont-ils pris mon logis?' "*

Then followed verse after verse, monotonous and stirring, like the sound of a running stream and the wind in the leaves. At last the trader's voice broke into a sort of cry and then died away like the voice of a dying man.

> *"Très sainte Vierge, ah! m'abandonnez pas,*
> *Permettez-moi d'mourir entre vos bras."*

The girl was crying quietly.

"She cry always when I sing that song," said the trader with satisfaction. "Cadreux, one day he come home. Far off he see smoke. 'Hé,' says he. 'The Iroquois, they burn my leetle house, hé?' Then he dying—he tell the wolf, he tell the black crow, 'Don' you eat me. You go eat the Iroquois I have killed.' Then he

51

think of hees frien's and hees young wife, so far away in that canoe all safe, and he tell the birds, 'You go say farewell.' He all alone. No one there to help heem die. Then he say, 'Holy virgin, do not you leave me, too— you let me die, please, between your arms.' "

Silence fell on the room. Seth felt the forests all about the clearing, the forests of the hunters and *coureurs-de-bois,* the trappers, and the *voyageurs* on the great rivers and the Iroquois lurking along the lonely trails, and over it all the lady in her blue mantle, her hands stretched out in compassion. He felt it vaguely and confusedly, more as an emotion than a complete vision, but something very different from the English villages with their forts and meeting houses and their fenced-in fields, and the life he had lived.

It was late. The sounds from the village had died away to the occasional barking of a dog. The squaw and the girl again took his hands and led him once more into the moonlight.

XI

THE FEAST

THE days that followed were busy ones for the squaws and captives. They set great kettles at the edge of the cornfields and kept fires burning under them all day long, while they boiled the ears of corn until the kernels were hard. Seth was busy bringing piles of wood for the fires; when he was not doing that, he was stripping back the green husks from the ears, or helping the squaws slit the bark from the elm trees to be used as trays on which to dry the kernels, which they scraped from the ears with clamshells. After the first half day he did not have John Hammond to help him, for the big man made very merry in the cornfield, by his pretended clumsiness upsetting a kettle filled with ears into the fire and tripping over the trays covered with the small precious kernels. The squaws went in a body for Natanis who came lowering, with Squint Eye at his elbow.

"This is squaw's work," said John Hammond grandly. "I am a man."

And in spite of Squint Eye's objections, John Hammond was allowed to leave the cornfield, and every day he grew more important in the eyes of the chiefs.

But Seth well knew that he was too young to be taken seriously. If he had tried to cut his cloth by John Hammond's, he would only have had a beating for it from Bedagi. And besides that, he really liked the work, for unconsciously it seemed like home to be getting in a harvest and storing it. The little kernels, they told him, would last for years and when they were boiled again they would turn sweet and as large as they had been on the ear. He often worked near Keoka, the girl who had helped him. She taught him the Indian names of things, and he taught her the English which she was very quick to learn, pronouncing her words swiftly and clearly with a slight singsong.

When all the corn had been dried and part of it buried in the Indian barns (as the English called the holes in the ground lined with bark which were used for storing provisions) and part of it put aside for each family to take with it during the winter's wanderings, a feast was given. Seth felt very strongly about the Indians' wastefulness with food, inviting all their friends in and gorging on whatever they had; and in the winter when food was so uncertain and life so precarious, he was to feel even more strongly about this custom. But a feast now at the end of harvest seemed natural to him, like the Thanksgiving days he had always known. All night long the women were busy pounding corn; and venison, corn, and beans were bubbling together in pots.

A crier went out calling: *"Kuh menscoorebah!"*—"I come to conduct you to a feast!"—at each door, and the man within answered, asking if he were to bring a knife or a spoon in his dish. "Both," said the crier each time, and soon the braves were assembled.

Seth was told to stand outside the door on one side and Keoka's grandmother stood on the other, shaking her hands, and dancing, her old wrinkled face filled with smiles as she sang, *"Wegage oh nelo woh!"*—"Fat is my eating! Fat is my eating!"

Seth also danced and sang though he made a face at John Hammond, going in to the lodge with the warriors.

When the men had been served, the crier appeared

at the door and called, and now from all parts of the town the women came hurrying with their wooden bowls for their share of the feast which each took back to her own wigwam to eat. Persis and Mrs. Snow did not come, but Keoka was there and laughed at both Seth and her grandmother, imitating their dancing in high spirits. When the women were gone again, the men sat about the lodge, each in turn telling tales of old hunts or wars, singing songs, or repeating legends. Seth remained at the entrance, his head resting against the frame of the house, the bowl heaped with Indian stew in his hands. He could not understand very much of what was being said inside, but the deep voices soothed him, and the sound of laughter, and when the old squaw who sat on the other side of the entrance caught his glance she smiled at him wisely and kindly.

"Good," she said in her own language, content in the moment, like a squirrel with a nut, Seth thought.

But he was English and could not forget the winter that lay before them, even there sitting in the late afternoon sunshine, drowsy with eating.

XII

THE GEESE FLY SOUTH

IT SEEMED as though the rain had held off only until the corn could be harvested, for now it rained and rained, day after day. Many of the leaves fell in the constant drip and one could see hills beyond the woods that had been invisible in the summer; the earth was soggy underfoot; the river rose, almost covering the light tidal strip at its banks; and by day and night the loons gave their wild call, signifying rain still to come.

Seth, whose duty it was to find wood, was wet all the time, and so for that matter were most of the others; for hunting and fishing must go on rain or shine, and the lodges were full of the steaming of wet blankets and the smell of drying wool and leather. The dogs, too, crowded into the shelter; Seth often woke in the night to find several lying on top of him in the narrow space where he curled, his feet to the fire. With five grown-up people and four children, there was little room in the wigwam, and worst of all was the smoke which the rain drove back from the vent hole and which filled the place with its choking fumes, smarting his throat and eyes. The smoke at least kept away the last mosquitoes and biting flies, but on the fleas it had no effect.

But Seth minded all this less than he had expected, and to his own surprise neither he nor the other white people seemed any the worse for their soakings. However, he did keep as close to the fire as he could, and more than once caught Bedagi's cuff for being slow to go out into the drizzle when ordered. There were many hours of enforced leisure, some of which he used in whittling himself a wooden fork with two tines at which Bedagi at first scoffed, declaring that it had horns like a snail. But later his master ordered one for himself, and so did the rest of the lodge, each making Seth some small present in return.

One morning Seth wakened to a different feel in the air. The patter of rain on the sides of the lodge which had been so constant was gone, the smoke of the fire rose straight through the vent hole, instead of being beaten back into his stinging eyes and nostrils; his blood tingled with the cold freshness of the air.

Stealing outdoors, he found all the world sparkling with a million raindrops flashing in the sun. Even in the rain, many of the maples and beeches had begun to change their color; now they shone in scarlet and wet gold, and the cornstalks that had been so green and stalwart were pale and frail as ghosts.

A perfect fury of hunting took the tribe and there were many feasts. Keoka took him with her one day after a deer. He was very much surprised, for he had never seen one of the women go hunting before.

"I am the only man in our lodge," she explained smiling. "Some day when I marry, my husband will hunt for us."

"I'll hunt for you today, Keoka," said Seth, but the girl shook her head, looking important and mischievous at the same time.

"You are only a captive boy," she said. "They would be angry, if I let you take the gun."

"But you are only a girl," said Seth. "You may be able to hunt rabbits and deer, but what can you do in winter, when the wolves are about and you must face the great ones of the forest?"

The girl bit her lip and then smiled. Leaning the gun against a tree, she pulled up her sleeve and showed her arm with a deep red scar where the flesh had been torn away.

"A bear," she said briefly. "Natanis killed him with his tomahawk."

"Are you not afraid?" asked Seth, awed.

"No," she said, "the bear's meat saved us. We were starving."

She pulled down her sleeve, and seeing his face, began to laugh.

"How can you laugh?" asked Seth.

"You look as though you were starving now," said Keoka. "There is plenty of corn, and there is the hunter's moon." She touched his arm. "If you live with us, you must learn to trust the Great Spirit for your food."

Later in the afternoon, he found that she was a very good shot. She killed a young stag, butchered the meat, and carried a load back to camp as heavy as he could carry, using all his strength. Later, she showed him how the meat was jerked, cutting it into long strips and drying it for the winter over a slow fire. Bit by bit, and chiefly through Keoka, he learned Indian ways.

Now every night was a night of frost, and the woods turned all ablaze. The Indians moved, bronze figures, between the gold and scarlet of hanging leaves and the gold and scarlet of the leaves fallen on the ground, and Seth was aware of a beauty in them that he scarcely admitted to himself. A great homesickness came over him, greater than any he had felt since he had been captured. The birds were passing, warblers and forest grosbeaks, bluebirds and red-breasted robins, all turning south. The Indians were preparing, too, for their migrations: the village was busy with the jerking of meat, the mending of skin clothes, the making of moccasins, and the packing of dried corn and beans. Everyone was going somewhere. Only the prisoners did not know where they were going and were false to the spirit of migration that fled by on every wind. Even the butter-flies were on the march. Seth came one late afternoon to a grove of sugar maples and stopped, astonished at the sight before him of thousands of butterflies flutter-ing from bough to bough, their wings the exact gold of the foliage, so that in that molten light the leaves them-selves seemed flying and fluttering.

All to himself he sang the wailing prisoner's song, "I don't know where I go." The very landscape, itself, added to his sense of desolation. It was not the varied red of the maples nor the yellow of the many birches that made Seth feel sick for home, but the small red of the wild strawberry leaves, and the starred bramble vines that ran close to earth and had so often caught at his bare ankles when he used to cross the home pasture to get Jenny; it was the purple-red of the low-bush blueberries, and the round bright red of the checker-berries under their green and glossy leaves in the woods, and the red of the robins' breasts—all these small and intimate scarlets of autumn pierced him with a sense of exile and set him wondering, inconsequentially, if his mother were letting Abigail wear the red muffler she had knitted for him.

And he made a solemn vow, alone, by the side of the river, that he would never give up trying to return home until he died.

Then one night the wild geese flew over the village. Seth woke to their call in the darkness, plucking at the heart with its one single wild note of challenge and exploration. Looking through the smoke hole, he thought the stars were for a moment darkened by the passing of great wings.

Bedagi spoke from the other side of the wigwam.

"Tomorrow we go."

XIII

KEOKA

THE Indians always deserted their villages during the winter, for there was not food enough then in any one locality to support more than one or two families. Breaking up into groups, they wandered through the woods, men, women, and little children, following the game, hunting and trapping as best they could until late spring brought them back to the cleared lands to plant their little fields of corn, sometimes in one village and again, as the fit took them, in another.

Bedagi's household filled two canoes, and as they were the first to leave, most of the town was down at the shore to see them off, many of them bringing with them presents. Seth had his share. Tardieu, the trader, gave him a fine knife over which everyone exclaimed.

63

"You like my song, hé, leetle English?" he asked. "I
bring you this knife—when you see eet, you think of
me and of that fine fellow, the trapper, eh?"

Mrs. Snow had made him a frilled shirt, "So that
you need not be ashamed, if they take you to Quebec,
Seth," she said wistfully.

All the other prisoners were dressed in fringed elk
and deerskin like Indians, now, but she still mended
her worn English clothes and refused to part with
them.

Persis tried to give him her doll, and Keoka brought
him two pairs of moccasins trimmed with dyed porcu-
pine quills.

"But they fit exactly!" Seth cried delightedly. "How
did you know the size of my feet, Keoka?"

"By the size of your footprints, O Chief," she said,
mocking him as she so often did, for she lived with
laughter.

John Hammond, too, teased him. "Here you go off
and leave Persis, Seth, after promising to take care of
her," he said. "Is that good behavior in an Englishman
of your excellent training?"

Seth half rose in the canoe.

"Don't be a fool, lad," cried John Hammond quickly.
"You must go where your master takes you. Mrs. Job
and her papoose and I are to hunt with Mrs. Snow's

master this winter. I shall look after them, God willing."

Seth looked at him, so tall even among the tall Indians and so sure of himself. Anyone would be safe
with John Hammond, he thought. He felt very much
alone, going away into the wilderness with the Indians.

But as the canoes were about to be pushed off, there
was a sudden outbreak of argument on the shore. Keoka
had turned and was passionately addressing her grandmother, now commanding, now beseeching, while the
crowd added to the confusion by joining in the discus-
sion in a babel of voices. From it all, Seth made out that
the girl was asking the old woman to agree to go with
Bedagi's family for the winter.

"But Natanis—" said the old squaw.

"But Bedagi—" cried the young one, and in the end
had her own way.

Her cheeks darkly glowing with excitement, her eyes
shining, the girl turned to the canoes which were still
waiting and asked permission for her grandmother and
herself to set their lodge beside Bedagi and his brother's
lodge.

The Indians, looking amused, agreed, and soon after
they had disembarked that evening and set up their
temporary shelters, Seth saw with pleasure a small
canoe paddled by the two women silently come to the

beach beside their canoes. That night a second shelter stood beside the other.

There began for Seth a curious, almost dreamlike, existence. The streams and lakes were filled with migrating ducks, wild geese, and great white swans. The deer and moose, intent on their affairs of mating, were easily killed, and even the dogs grew fat. Slowly the bright colors faded and most of the leaves turned to various shades of fawn and brown.

"Look, Keoka," said Seth one day. "The woods were dressed in feathers. Now they have laid them aside and are dressed in leather."

"It is a poem!" said Keoka and began chanting his words.

"The woods were dressed in feathers,
 I yeh, i yeh, i yeh!
 They have laid aside their feathers and are clad in
   leather,
 I yeh, i yeh, i yeh!"

She sang the song to the other Indians that night.

"The little English make it," she said, and from that time on Seth had something of a reputation as a poet and was called upon for songs at feasts. But as these songs were only a line long, he did not find his task very difficult.

Now came Indian summer, and the days had an un-
natural warmth and stillness, almost as though wizards
had cast a spell over them. Seth was never told where
they were going and found his pack very heavy,
now, in the warmth, for they had buried the canoes by
the river and traveled inland, following the streams.
He often lagged behind the others and found himself
walking alone through the woods in which the last
oak leaves hung brown in the blue haze of naked
branches. And then he would imagine that he saw
church spires beyond the trees and heard the noise of a
distant city, and he would think to himself: "Tonight
we will be in Quebec, or perhaps Montreal. The forest
is growing opener. Soon we shall be coming upon the
farms."

But always the forest went on, pines and spruce and
firs, maples, beeches and oaks, moss, ferns and berries,
and always he slept on the ground in his dirty blanket,
his feet to a small fire whose sticks he, himself, had
gathered though his shoulders ached with the weight
of the load he had carried on them all day.

"If Bedagi would only say where he was going,"
Seth said bitterly to Keoka one day as he sat by her side
a little off from the others, each with a wooden bowl
heaped full of meat and beans, for the hunting had been
good.

67

"It is not important," replied Keoka indifferently.

"But it *is* important," said Seth. "You do not understand. An Englishman wishes to know where he is going."

Keoka hummed the prisoner's song, then seeing that he was serious, added quietly, "But I do not know either. One place is much like another. Bedagi watches for signs of game and above all obeys the dreams that he has by night. Day by day, he chooses from such things."

"But what do you gain in the end by all this crisscrossing?" cried Seth again.

"We live," said Keoka. "You do not yet understand how difficult that is."

"Then why do they all use up what they have when they have it? Now, for instance, this is more than I can eat," and taking out a piece of meat from his bowl, he prepared to wrap it up and put it in his pouch.

But Keoka, who had eaten her own large share, took it from his hand and ate his piece also. Then she licked her fingers carefully, took a twig and scratched in the earth three marks like a bird alighting on the ground.

Y

"That," she said, "means in our picture language

'now'— the instant of a bird's touching the earth before his wings are folded. So do we live, feast when we feast, starve when we starve."

Seth started to interrupt her, but she motioned him to be silent until she had finished.

"You English with your barns of hay and your barrels of flour, with your cows and the cabbages in the cellar, what do you know of hunger or uncertainty? Your cattle graze over the Indians' bones; the loud noises of your bells and your guns scare away the game. When we come to spear fish or gather mussels at the entrances of the rivers, your forts fire upon us. We are driven from our best hunting grounds. You buy our beaver skins and make us drunk with your brandy; you make treaties and break them; you seize upon our chiefs at the sacred council fires themselves. We are driven back into the hills to live as best we can. Yet we are nearer the Great Spirit than you are. He feeds us with a kind hand, giving us corn and beans. We lean against His knee and He gives us meat in the snow. You English go to church on the Sabbath and think that your food comes from your own skill, but we are fed by the Great Spirit each day and give thanks to Him with every meal. When He withholds food from us, it is to remind us that it is upon Him we depend. We sup from the bowl He extends to us, and it is ingrati-

tude to weigh and hoard like an ungrateful guest eye-
ing the dishes at a feast."

A leaf fell into the girl's lap as she finished speaking,
like a sort of period to her words. Seth sat silent, and
in his mind, which was always one that saw life in
images, there rose glimpses of his mother washing their
clothes at the spring and the clean white of linen
stretched on the grass to dry; and he saw his father with
his arms full of the sheaves which he was stacking late
in the afternoon, still untired; and he heard the mill
grinding its grain slowly between the great stones where
the tidewater bubbled and saw the congregation rise
orderly to sing in the cold white austerity of the meeting house. There was something here that made use of
the land deeply, that became part of it. Surely those
hayfields and cornfields, the bearded barley and the
rich meadows with the grazing cattle should not go
back to the wilderness so that an Indian might kill a
deer there once in a year, perhaps. All this he felt as
passionately as she had felt, but he could not find words
for it in his own language, much less in a strange
tongue.

"You would understand, if you were English," he
muttered.

"But I *am* English!" she cried.

XIV

HUNGER

THE wind veered into the northeast, and Indian summer was forgotten. A snow fell heavy, white, and wet, bending down the evergreen branches, breaking the ferns, mounding the bushes, turning the world to white, black, and green-black on silver. The sunsets were lemon colored now behind a tracery of branches and dark spires of pines sliced with white; the great hunter with his scalping knife at his belt strode the night skies, and wolves came near their encampments in the darkness, leaving rings of doglike footprints where they had circled the smell of fire and the smell of food. The days were very short.

Seth faced the winter with strung nerves, like an enemy whom he must outwit if he were ever to return to his own fireside; but at first there did not seem much to face. The cold was not extreme, and in spite of his thin clothing he kept warm enough. When they moved from one camp to another, the men cleared away the snow with their snowshoes, while the women cut long boughs for a framework on which to wrap their coverings of bark and skins. The ground within the wigwam and the snow outside they strewed with hemlock boughs, and slept with their feet to the fire and their heads to the snow bank. All the dogs slept with them, now more than ever, and Seth was glad of their warmth all about him. When it snowed the smoke was very bad, and it took Seth a long time to become used to the melted snow water, drunk warm, from the bowls that tasted of grease and smoke. But he was not one to think more than he could help of difficulties and he greatly enjoyed other aspects of the life, such as the snowshoeing.

"Canoes in summer, snowshoes in winter—Indian's horse," said Bedagi.

For some time the hunting seemed easier than ever, and now on the white sheet of the snow Seth learned something of the art of tracking: he learned to tell in a moment where the deer had bedded; to distinguish a bull moose from a cow moose by the width of the hoof-marks, and an old moose from a young one by the clarity of the outline of the track; he learned that the female bear hibernates in trees where she has her young, and the male under roots or in caves; he learned to hunt beavers in their wigwams and enjoy the delicious broth made from their tails; his eyes grew keen to recognize the tracks of the little masked raccoons who hid, four or five together, in the hollow trees; and he could tell at a sniff the musky smell of a fox from the old odor of skunk, sweet as rotten grapes.

He was told other things that he doubted in spite of Bedagi's faith—that the wild geese turn into beavers in the fall, for instance, or that rattlesnakes change into raccoons. All the Indian tales were thick with accounts of magicians who continually changed from one form to another, in escaping or outwitting their enemies by their manifold shapes. Walking watchful through the woods where a stump might seem a bear, or a bear might seem a stump, where the trees groaned against one another like spirits in pain, and the wind reached out to wipe away a hunter's tracks behind him, even

Seth came to understand the feeling that the solitary Indians had of moving through a world highly conscious of their presence, watched by many strange eyes they did not see.

In fact, during those first few weeks the woods were a continual enchantment to Seth.

"It will be a long winter," said Bedagi. "See, the bees build high. They expect much snow. And both bees and squirrels have laid up a great store of food."

But the words had no warning for Seth. Here they were, living in the winter he had dreaded, and it was nothing very terrible. True, all the geese and swans and the ducks, too, were gone, even the loons that waited until the ponds froze. Only the blue jays, crested and brilliant as birds embroidered with beads, sat and scolded on the boughs, shaking down soft showers of snow that made snow rainbows in the sunlight. Only the white owl veered past them on the edge of night.

The hominy they had brought was all gone, eaten generously while it lasted. Now, while the men hunted, the women gathered a few acorns and nuts. Seth scarcely noticed that the game was not as plentiful as it had been at first. A warm day had melted the snow, and a cold night had frozen it again. Now there was a crackling crust that warned all creatures of the wood that an enemy was coming, no matter with what care a hunter stepped. Seth began to learn what it was to go hungry to a cold bed, but it was not until after the blizzard that he knew what winter and hunger really meant.

All day and night it snowed heavily, unhurriedly. The next morning they had to dig themselves out from their lodges. The world was sparkling white under a blue sky and intensely cold. Nothing stirred anywhere. There were no tracks.

The Indians began eating their dogs. Keoka cried when her favorite had to be killed, but she ate him with the rest, though the tears ran down her face. Seth came and sat beside her and put his hand on her knee, saying nothing, as he did not know what to say. The dog had always seemed to him an ugly scarred brute who often growled at his heels and was always being scolded by Keoka or her grandmother, but now he saw that she had loved him.

Keoka stroked his hand, gratefully. Ever since she had told him that she was English, she had been shy with him, and when he had asked her questions, she had only said that she did not know; it had all happened a long time ago. She was very sorry that she had told him her secret: as an Indian girl, she was one thing; as a white woman, turned Indian, she was dimly afraid she was another. Seth, looking at her now, was surprised

75

that he had never guessed her race, but then, she was naturally dark and lithe. She was growing thin; he saw plainly her cheekbones, and the small bones of her wrists. He kept wondering where she had come from and who she really was. She was like the taste of wild plum jam, tart and sweet, compared to the girls he had known, and in his heart he made a second vow—that she should not die an Indian.

But in the days to follow, death came hourly nearer Bedagi's encampment. The deer and moose had gone into their yards, herding together in trampled circles from which they rarely stirred, getting what food they could by slowly enlarging the circles to include more and more browse. The blizzard had wiped out their tracks, and lucky would a hunter be who might come upon their winter refuges.

Keoka snared a rabbit. The whole party, seven adults and four children, each had his scrupulously fair share of the meat. Even the squirrel that Seth knocked down with a stick was divided among them all. Now they took the fox and deer bones the dogs had once gnawed, and which still lay about, and broke them open between stones and made a broth from them. A raccoon made a feast over which they all licked their chops. Three days went by and they had only bark to chew; Keoka walked with a stick. She had secretly saved most of her share of the raccoon for her grandmother. The children were crying with hunger, and Seth felt light headed as he took Keoka's gun and went off into the woods.

"Surely," he thought, "surely today I will find something. Something will move, something will stir."

But nothing in the wilderness stirred, save Seth himself. At night he returned, following his own snowshoe track, stumbling wearily to the encampment.

"Broth, my brother!" called Keoka cheerfully, at the door of her wigwam. "Bring thy bowl and spoon."

The others were all there, drinking the broth. He glanced at the hunters. They shook their heads. They had killed nothing. The broth was hot snow water with a faint flavor of something else, a faint rank odor. Whatever it was, it was very weak, but the heat gave him a little cheer.

When he had finished, he asked, "What have we tasted, my sister?"

She laughed.

"It is moccasin broth," she said. "My best moccasins, flavored with the fringes of my skirt. How do you like our fare, my brother?"

"Good fare in a bad time," he answered gravely.

The next day there was nothing but more moccasin broth, and an elkskin thong that he chewed all day.

The next day Bedagi and his brother and Seth killed

a moose. Somehow, the beast happened to be out from his yard; somehow, as they followed him, he blundered into a swamp; circling it, they found no trace of his departure from it; entering it, they came upon him with a broken leg caught in a tangle of roots. Quickly they killed him, quickly built a high platform where the bulk of the meat would be safe from the wolves, and quickly they brought three loads of the best home on their backs. The squaws took pieces of it and began broiling them on green spits. The odor filled Bedagi's wigwam, and a scarecrow child snatched at a chunk and crammed it almost raw into his mouth.

"You have done ill, my son," said Bedagi above the pipe he was serenely smoking. "We have waited long. To wait a little longer, now, until the meat is done is nothing. Let us eat of the gift of the Great Spirit like men and not like wolves."

XV

TALES BY THE FIRE

SETH'S will to return home had never faltered, but his inner certainty had been shaken in the last few days before the moose was killed. Now, sitting by the fire, the empty bowl in his hand, it rose in him again.

"Some day all this will be like a dream which I will tell them at Pemaquoit," he thought drowsily.

Bedagi and his brother were smoking; the women and children sat quietly, their eyes fixed on the flames. No one had been allowed to eat much. They had been too near starvation for that, but each had had enough to bring him a new strength and hope. Seth looked toward Keoka, and she smiled back at him from where she sat beside the wrinkled squaw whom she called her grandmother.

It was Bedagi's brother who laid aside his pipe and began speaking slowly.

"Beyond the headwaters of the Penobscot rise the blue heights of Katahdin which no man save me has ever lived to climb, for it is the abode of the giant wizard Pamola. One spring I had my lodge by the river and every day, looking up from the fire, I saw Katahdin's blue crest through the smoke vent. I was a young man then, proud of my strength, and one morning, saying nothing to my wife here, I set off toward the mountain. At dusk I built my fire in the shelter of a cliff, and soon afterwards a terrible storm arose. The thunder and lightning were continual, trees fell all about me, and the rain came down heavy as the fall of the great cataract of Niagara. Then, knowing that no man could live through such a night, I took all my tobacco and laid it on the last of my fire and I called upon Pamola himself to come and save me. With his first step the mountain rocked. With his second step he stood by my fire. He had the feet of an eagle and the head of a moose, but his eyes were the eyes of a wildcat.

" 'It is you, O my brother,' I said, though my teeth rattled.

" 'You are wise to have called me by that name,' he bellowed. 'If you had not, I should have killed and eaten you, too.'

"Then he set me upon his shoulder and in two steps he brought me to the door of his lodge which fills the inside of the mountain. We entered. There was a fire, and there sat his squaw and their children. The sides of the wigwam were of solid stone. They put me by the fire and fed me as one feeds a guest, with venison and fat sweetened with maple syrup, and with corn cakes. When he had finished, Pamola said: 'Now I shall give a dance in your honor.'

" 'Who will dance?' I asked, seeing only the woman and her children.

" 'The dancers will come,' he said, fastening two great rocks onto his clawed feet with thongs.

"Then he began to sing, beating the time, striking the rocks on his feet against the rocky floor of his wigwam until all the mountain throbbed like a drum of stone. Then came the dancers out of the darkness of the wigwam. They were skeletons, and as long as Pamola beat the time the skeletons danced and I saw the firelight shining through their ribs.

"In the morning Pamola carried me back to where he had found me and disappeared. On my shoulder I found one of the little hairs from his cheek."

He opened a pouch by his side and drew forth a small roll of doeskin from which he took a black strong hair more than three feet long. The children gazed at it with wonder, and even Seth was so under the spell of the story that he scarcely listened to that part of his mind which said: "It looks like a hair from a horse's tail."

It was Keoka who asked for a song, she who always loved singing. Bedagi looked at her kindly.

"My daughter," he said, "you are nearly ready now for marriage, and I will sing the love song that the young man sings when he leaves the woman he loves, as their households separate for the winter hunting, bidding her look for his return."

The words of the song were very simple, but the melody was full of tenderness and a sense of something coming:

> *"Look oft up the river, look oft and oft,*
> *In spring at the breaking of the ice, look oft;*
> *You may see me coming down in my canoe.*
> *Look oft up the river, look oft and oft.*
> *Ku we nu de nu,*
> *Ku we nu de nu."*

XVI

THE HOLLOW TREE

AFTER the killing of the moose, the encampment was never again during the winter in real danger of starvation; but Seth often enough went hungry, and the hunters were thin with ranging the woods after food and peltry. For this was the time of the year when each lodge laid up a store of beaver and fox and marten and muskrat skins to exchange in the spring with the traders for the things they needed. The beaver skins were the most important. They were the unit of exchange. One skin was worth a brass kettle, or one and a half pounds of gunpowder, five pounds of shot, one pound of Brazil tobacco, or one gallon of brandy. These were the things the Indians most wanted, but often enough the traders gave them the brandy first and then got the skins for almost nothing. Seth learned how to take beaver in their houses that looked like wigwams, and how to make and set traps. His carrying muscles grew strong under heavy loads of skins, for each time they moved to a new place they must carry their peltry, often making many trips back and forth before the last skin was in its place on the new scaffolding.

Seth, too, was thin, but more untiring than he had ever been, and now he moved warily, never forgetting his respect for the forest and for winter, those two sorcerers so expert in changing their forms. Despite his care, however, he had one more terrifying experience at their hands. They had set up a camp on a stream in the vicinity of several ponds that Bedagi said were rich in beaver. A very tall pine tree made an open space under its branches, and here stood the large wigwam of Bedagi and his brother and the small one of Keoka's grandmother. There was a spring near the spot and several game trails led to it, which one might follow into rolling country, from whose heights one saw distant mountains to the north, beyond which Bedagi said lay the great St. Lawrence and Quebec.

One day, Seth had been out hunting by himself and

had gone farther than he intended. When he turned, it was already late afternoon, and he knew that he must hurry. The tracks of his snowshoes made a clear trail that tied him like a cord to the safety of the lodges, and he began following it at an easy run. He had not gone far, however, when it began to snow, a thing he had not expected in the least, and a teasing small wind crept over the crust, blowing the new snow into the depressions made by his snowshoes. At first, he could still trace them by the difference in texture, but soon this became impossible in the failing light. He lost the trail, blundered panic stricken, found it again, followed it a hundred yards and lost it once more. Like a fool, he had come away without tinder and he had never, even in dry weather, succeeded in making a fire from two sticks as the Indians could do.

If he were not to become hopelessly lost and freeze to death during the night, he knew he must keep his head and work quickly, or he would never see his family and Pemaquoit again.

The thought steadied him. Abandoning any attempt to follow the lost trail, he wandered at random, his eyes keenly observing the old trees. Now the Forest played into his hand, taking his part for the moment against the other sorcerer Winter, for within a few minutes he came upon what he was looking for, a large hollow tree with an entrance low enough for him to climb in. He found himself in a cavern about three feet in diameter and high enough to stand upright in; best of all, it was still dry.

Near Seth's tree lay a fallen spruce and to this he went, chopping off the upper branches with the ax he carried in his belt, until he had a protection three or four feet deep stacked about the entrance of his hollow, leaving only a small opening by which to squeeze in. He also put small branches in the hollow and arranged a large piece of wood, fastened with a thong, with which to block the entrance when he was once in.

It was very exciting, closing his cavern, pulling the block in place, and filling the cracks with the twigs until no faint sliver of the twilight reached him. Then with his ax he tore down all the rotten wood he could reach into a soft dry floor, and taking off his soaking moccasins, danced for half an hour, up and down, up and down, until his feet and his whole body tingled with warmth. He had only his moccasins, his leggings, breechclout, and blanket, but he had often been colder in his bed under the eaves on a winter night than he was when he lay curled in the heart of the tree, his blanket about him, and his moccasins under his head to keep them from freezing.

Sometime during the night he woke in the darkness

and lay listening to the storm outside, feeling safe in his shelter. The next time he woke, he felt sure it must be day, but no glimmer of light entered the hollow tree. It took him some time to find with his hands where the block had been wedged in, and when he did, it refused to give. Suddenly, the darkness became horrible to him. His shelter turned into a trap. For a wild minute, he saw himself dying in this remorseless tree, a death more terrible than the storm would have given him. But after resting a few minutes he again threw his weight against the block, and this time it moved and a quantity of snow fell in upon him with the blessed light of the outside world.

Hastily putting on his moccasins again and belting his blanket about him, he climbed out of his shelter.

He had never before seen such a snow. Three feet, at least, it had fallen in a single night, and the branches of the evergreens, bowed with its weight, touched the white ground in endless arches as far as he could see. The sun was hidden still by gray clouds, but he remembered Bedagi's teachings.

"In general," he had often told the boy, "the tops of pine trees lean toward the rising sun; moss grows toward the roots of trees on the side which faces north; and the limbs are largest and most numerous on the side which faces south."

When one sign failed, Seth used another. He made slow work of it, but he knew the general direction of the camp, and when in the afternoon he reached a stream, he was certain that he had only to follow it down to come upon the Indians. He was not certain whether the encampment lay a few yards or miles downstream; actually, he discovered it was not far.

The two lodges were in an uproar of rejoicing at his return. Keoka began to cry—she who had never cried when hunger laid its bony hand upon her. Bedagi, who had spent most of the day hunting for him, made a formal speech of welcome and praise for his resourcefulness.

"My son," he added, "it was all that we could do to keep Keoka from trying to find you in the night and storm. I had myself to hold her. She would have died within an hour."

Seth, very much moved, sat down to a dish of stew that smelled more delicious to him than any food he had ever tasted on his mother's carefully scrubbed table in the freshly sanded kitchen at home.

But his pleasure was marred by discovering that the fine knife which Tardieu the trader had given him was lost. It was the only thing he had which was really his own; and the others all admired it and envied him for it. He must have lost it at the hollow tree, he thought. Bedagi, seeing his disappointment, immediately rose and picked up his gun.

"I will go get it for you," he said. "Your tracks will be plain to follow."

He had been out since early morning searching the woods. Seth's first protest was sincerely for Bedagi's sake. Then a memory of Mrs. Snow's feather beds stuffed with booty on the backs of Indians swept before his eyes. Bedagi wanted the knife, he thought. If he found it, he would keep it for himself.

Closing his lips in a straight line, Seth said nothing more, and Bedagi strapped on his snowshoes and disappeared from sight.

Just after sunset, when the trees were sinking back into the night, and the wigwams looked like huddling darkness, Bedagi returned and gave the knife to Seth.

They had lived through the hunger together; they had tramped and hunted together over many miles; Bedagi had, at the time of his capture, several times saved Seth's life; but it was with the touch of the knife that the Indian had gone so far to bring back to him that the first real feeling of friendliness came into Seth's heart.

"Thank you, my uncle," he said, using the Indian title of courtesy which he had never used before.

And from that evening on he began to excuse even the cruelty he had witnessed among the Indians, by remembering the difference in their form of life and bringing-up, and the wrongs they had suffered.

XVII

A Stranger Arrives

Not long after this event, while they were still at the same encampment, they had a visitor. One afternoon when Keoka was sitting beside Seth in her lodge, each busy making a trap with wood strengthened in the fire, she raised her head, listening.

"What is it?" she asked.

Seth listened and heard nothing.

"A wood spirit," he said, mocking her.

But she kept her intent frown.

"No, it is someone," she answered and, rising, gave a

clear ringing call from the door of the lodge and then bent to fasten on her snowshoes.

"Come with me, my brother," she said as she did so, "and hurry. In winter one never can tell in what need the newcomer may be. His shout seemed to me faint, and not far off."

"It is only a ringing in your ears or the cry of a blue jay," said Seth, but he hurried into his own snowshoes and followed her down the game trail along their stream. When they had gone a little distance, the girl hallooed again, and this time Seth, too, heard the answer.

"It is a white man," said Keoka over her shoulder as she broke into a sort of trot, and Seth's heart leaped.

"A white man after all these months," he thought, wondering who it could be, for no white trappers came so far south, and the traders followed the rivers in canoes in the spring and waited at the Indian towns.

A prisoner like himself, escaped? Then Bedagi must not know. He hurried after Keoka, and now it seemed to him that she was going all too slowly. Even as it was she checked herself to call again, but this time the feeble answer came from near by, a little to the left.

Whoever it was was in trouble.

Over Keoka's shoulder he saw a tall man stooped un-der a sort of small but heavy chest which he carried on his back. He wore a brown gown whose skirts were thick with snow, and quiet dark eyes looked at them from a middle-aged face, white and drawn with pain. The stranger raised his hand, and unconsciously Seth bowed his head.

"Blessed be God," said the priest in the Indian tongue, "who has sent you, my children."

He staggered.

"It is Father Simon!" Keoka cried. "Take his other arm, Seth. He has been frostbitten."

The man smiled patiently at her.

"It is the little English maid," he said. "I thought you were Indians at first."

When they got him to the lodges, the squaws stripped his feet of their coverings and rubbed them, as well as his hands, with snow, while Keoka went out to find fir balsam, which she heated carefully in a clamshell on the fire and rubbed in the open wounds of the frostbites. Meantime, Father Simon had been given broth to drink, and when he had been made as comfortable as possible, he rolled into a blanket and went to sleep, one arm flung over the iron-bound chest he had carried.

He awoke in the mid-afternoon, when the hunters happened to return, and immediately asked the Indians to build him an altar under the great pine that roofed their clearing.

"The wigwam is too dark and filled with the smell of cooking," he said. "I love to hold mass under the open sky."

In spite of the protests of the Indians, who were against his standing on his feet, he opened the chest and drew forth an altar cloth and stole heavily embroidered with gold and green, as well as two small silver candlesticks and a silver goblet.

So in the snow, under the snow-encrusted boughs, Seth for the first time, standing beside Keoka, heard the solemn ritual of the mass, and stood with bowed head while the others knelt about him at the raising of the host.

Seth could not keep his eyes from the rich embroidery and gold lace of the stole and altar cloth, so unlike anything he had known in his sober bringing-up. Under the trees they seemed beautiful and strangely in place.

Father Simon, who noticed his interest, called him to the altar as he put away the beautiful things upon it.

"See," he said, "these embroideries were made for the Mission of the Penobscot by great ladies of the French court. That lily the queen, herself, made with her own hands. The candles are made of moose tallow and bayberries and are pleasant as incense; the wine I offer does not come from France, but is pressed from the wild grapes of the wilderness. You see, I am sent to redeem the souls of a savage race."

The priest seemed to think, and a look of happiness spread over his face.

"I am a plain man," he said gently, his hands resting on the folded altar cloth, "but I will tell you of a vision that came to me, unworthy as I am. Once I was lost as you see me now, but it was worse, much worse, for I was nearly snowblind as well, and I was very near death when I saw a light moving toward me among the trees. When it grew nearer, I saw that it was Our Lady. Her feet did not touch the snow; there were wild roses under them, and a crown of oak leaves rested upon her brow; and Our Lord, whom she carried, held in His arms a rabbit that looked at me with bright inquisitive eyes. Then leaning against His mother's breast, Our Lord smiled at me and opened His arms and the rabbit leaped to the snow. The vision faded before my eyes, but the rabbit remained, slowly moving before me as I followed, and it was he who led me back to the encampment."

After the evening meal, the priest asked if there were an Englishman called Long Chief with them.

"No," said Bedagi, "but he was taken with this boy and is his friend."

"I wish to give him warning," said the priest. "This

fall I was busy on the lower river and did not reach the upper villages until very late. I am now on my way to Quebec to see my superior, and I had as a guide a man named Tarumkin—"

"Squint Eye," said Seth under his breath, but the priest heard him.

"Yes," he said, smiling. "Well, he got drunk at a trader's house and kept making threats of what he would do to this big Englishman. When he was sober, I reasoned with him. You know I do not preach against the attacks on the English settlements, for they are built on ground stolen from the tribes. But I do preach against cruelty. One day he said to me: 'Say another word and I will leave you.' But I had to speak as God bade me, so he left me."

The priest paused, smiling ruefully. He thought for a while. "He took his gun and all our provisions," he added at last, simply, and went on, "The Lord in His infinite kindness showed me where a squirrel had hidden his little hoard. I took half and so lived to follow a game trail and find you."

Seth had always loved courage. He loved swaggering John Hammond; and he came to love Father Simon. But even for his sake he would not be convinced when in the next days the Franciscan sought to talk to him of his religion.

"Father Simon," he said at last, "more than all else in heaven or earth, I long for home and to be among my own people."

The priest put his hand on the boy's shoulder gently and looked into his eyes. "We will talk no more of these high matters, my son," he said. "Tell me your father's name and where you were taken and I will let the authorities in Quebec know in whose lodge you are, in case anyone attempts to redeem you."

A week later, when he was pronounced by the Indians ready for travel, Father Simon shouldered his strong box and turned north. Bedagi's brother went with him as guide, leaving only one seasoned hunter in the camp. But the spring was almost at hand.

XVIII

By the Broken Beaver Dam

SETH and Keoka were hunting beaver together, but when at last they found a dam it had been already broken into and the beavers taken.

"I should like to be like the young hunter who lived and feasted with the beavers all winter," said Keoka.

"What you ought to wish," said Seth, "is to have a decent woolen dress and an apron, a cap for your hair, a feather bed to lie on and a good husband to take you to meeting."

As he spoke he was chewing a twig, unconsciously noticing that it had lost its winter brittleness, though to the eye winter seemed as strong as ever.

Keoka flared back at him as he had meant she should.

"I wouldn't be one of your prim misses for anything,

tied to her pots and pans and the cradle, never wetting her shoe, or really seeing the sky. No, I shall marry an Indian and you can come to see us exchange the deer's leg and the ear of red corn, since he will keep me in meat and I will keep him in meal. I shall carry my baby through the woods and hang his cradle on a bough to swing in the wind. I don't want to be trapped in a house, my brother!"

And to his great surprise, she began to cry.

He, himself, was upset by the talk which had begun in fun.

"I don't care whether houses are traps or not," he said, catching hold of her hands quite roughly. "But where I go, you will go."

He did not quite know what he meant himself, but Keoka stopped crying and looked at him.

"Winter is almost over," she said, changing the subject. "It is time now for sugaring."

"There!" he exclaimed. "The Indians work with the seasons just as the whites do: peltries in winter; sugaring in spring; corn in summer; jerking meat in fall. How is that different from our way of living.

"It isn't in one place," said Keoka.

"It would be better if it were!" cried Seth.

Then they stuck out their tongues at each other, like small children.

Sugaring began in earnest now. The squaws with Seth to help them stripped bark from the elm trees and made crude buckets to help in gathering the sap. They had two great kettles that stood over the fires all the time. Seth loved the flames in the snow and the clear sap running out of the tomahawk gashes in the trees. With his French knife he whittled crude spigots, instead of the chips which the Indians commonly used to carry the sap away from the trunk so that it might drip into the buckets, and was greatly commended by the squaws. He noticed to his delight that the lichens on old stumps were covered with tiny coral-colored caps. The snow was beginning to melt close to the ground, out of sight; the ice on the streams was mottled now, in gray and white; and the tops of the budless trees had a rosy flush against the sky. They dipped their meat now in bear's fat in which maple sugar had been melted, and the little children grew round again and were noisy and quarrelsome as young puppies.

"No! No!" the squaws would say. "Be good, or you will be ducked in the stream," but the squaws were smiling even when they scolded.

The same restlessness which had come over the tribe in the fall was on them again. Even Seth felt it. He was always whistling tunelessly under his breath, moving about, watching the sky.

It was Seth who saw the first wedge of wild geese following their leader northward. And that night he awoke to hear Bedagi and his wife talking in low voices and knew that they were planning where that year they would plant their corn.

XIX

THE DREAM

NEXT morning Bedagi told the rest that they would spend the summer at St. Francis de Sales, near Quebec.

"I have never been there," said Keoka. "It is a new mission established for the Indians of the Penobscot and Kennebec, and there will be a Jesuit there and palisades for fear of the Mohawks. It is near the mouth of the Chaudière, below a fine falls, they say, and we shall live in a house. Then you will learn to eat eels, Seth! Everyone on the St. Lawrence eats eels winter and summer and I shall have an eelskin dyed red to tie back my hair."

"What is more important than your hair, my sister," said Seth, "is whether the others will be there or not."

"I think they will," said Keoka. "The captives will

wish to be near Quebec. It is such a fine city, Seth! I have passed it going to Trois-Rivières."

From that day the hunting party continually worked northward through the quickening woods, over low mountains, camping beside ponds or on the banks of northward-hurrying streams, until at last at the mouth of the Rivière du Loup, they struck the pale copper immensity of the St. Lawrence, which they followed westward in the canoes they had made on the Rivière du Loup, sometimes camping by the shore and once or twice staying in the house of a French habitant, where they were welcomed with kindness. It was in one of these houses, while lying in a real bed, having eaten food well seasoned with salt and served with bread, that Seth was troubled by a dream of John Hammond who appeared to him with half of his face blackened, and made him a gesture of the head, whether of welcome or of farewell, Seth waking in the darkness could not have said.

Next morning, when they had thanked the French family who had entertained them and were once more in their canoes, Seth told his dream to Bedagi.

"Perhaps Long Chief is sick," said the Indian. "Black on the face is the color of mourning; it is also the color with which prisoners are painted who are to die. But only half his face was painted. The dream was not final. Still, it is not lucky."

From living so long with the Indians, Seth had come to attach great importance to dreams. He had known of many instances when they had dreamed of game in a certain place and had next day found it there.

Sighing, he dipped his paddle in the yellow current, wondering if he should find John Hammond at St. Francis that evening. But soon his vague fears were soothed by the enormous width and smoothness of the river flowing all about him. The fog was settling down over the abrupt headlands and rolling shores, and through the misty half-light he saw the white porpoises lazily, slowly turning their sides to the surface in gleaming crescents like moons. Wherever the porpoises were, the sea gulls gathered, shining white with black tips to their wings, taking his heart back to the long summer days at Pemaquoit.

Their canoe, as usual, took the lead, its birch bark gleaming in the faint spring sunshine. The other canoes were less beautiful, being made of elm bark in the Iroquois fashion, since they had been in haste when they built them and birch trees of sufficient size had been hard to find. Seth always remembered the beauty of that especial day, and the sound of a church bell ringing from an unseen village.

Toward evening, the fog dissipated as quickly as it had gathered. And Seth had his first view of Quebec by sunset, a yellow unveiled sun whose low beams turned all the windows to flame. The fort lay on the height of the rock, and the city—churches, houses, stores, streets, and warehouses—seemed to have slipped from that height, trailing its weight across the face of the cliff, to lie with one end coiled at its base beside the river like a heavy wampum belt of stone patterned with fire. Here other canoes passed them, some filled with Indians and some with river men in their bright shirts. Bedagi was unwilling to make an unnoticed arrival at St. Francis after dark, so pulling their canoes to shore they prepared their fires once more on the shingle as the evening star brightened from the ashes of the sunset.

Next morning they arrived at St. Francis de Sales. Seth, hearing Bedagi give the prisoner whoop, became unpleasantly aware that he probably faced running the gantlet again. He had lived so long intimately with the Indians that the idea of rough handling from them came like cold water dashed in his face. However, here under the eyes of the priest, the thing was more a form than anything else. There was much laughter, but little pain. He had often felt sorer after a thrashing from his own father.

And now his friends crowded about him. Bedagi's brother shook him by the hand, grinning. "Father Simon has gone back to his river," he told him. "No, he is not lame."

Little Persis, looking scrawny but healthy, flung herself into his arms.

"We came here, too," she cried, speaking the Indian tongue, and looking like any of the other children except for her fair tousled hair and blue eyes.

"Dear," said her mother, "speak to Seth in English. Seth, I am glad you are safe. I have prayed for you often and often during this dreadful winter. If it had not been for John Hammond, we should all have died."

"Is he here?" Seth asked eagerly. "Is he well?"

She smiled her smile that brought back the youth to her face.

"He is very well," she said. "He is hunting now. But Mrs. Job has married again. Only last week we ate bear's meat for the wedding feast and Tarumkin is here, too, and still hates us."

She looked ill, white, and haggard; over her Indian dress she still wore an apron patched but clean.

Her eyes followed his glance. "I know it is foolish. I saved it all winter. Oh, Seth! I hate it all, the dirt and the fleas and the terrible things I have eaten which I would not have given to a dog. If it were not for

Persis' sake, I should have died long ago. I would rather be in my grave than living among savages."

She was silent. He saw her thin hand picking at her apron. When she looked up, her eyes were full of tears.

"And Persis is forgetting her English," she said, with infinite sadness in her voice.

Two of the prisoners whom he had known on the Penobscot in the fall were also there. The others had gone back to the coast with their masters, they said. One had died during the winter, struggling behind the Indians on the march. When they had gone back next morning, he was lying frozen, with a dog frozen in his arms.

"Ah, well," said one of the men, "there are worse deaths. It will do us no harm to learn how to live off the country for a few months. When I go back to my farm, I shall know a good deal more about keeping fresh meat on the table without killing my own stock, and laying up some peltry into the bargain to buy my wife a new gown now and then."

"Is there any talk of exchange or redeeming us?" Seth asked.

"There's always talk," said the man, "but nothing comes of it. Some say that a commission will come this summer by way of Albany. I don't know. Ask the priest."

Father de la Pré was a young man, thin, hook nosed, and painfully shy, dressed in the black of the Jesuits. He spoke to Seth without looking at him directly, in an English hesitating—like everything else about him —but correct, inquiring where he had been taken and when.

"Ah," he said, "then you were with Madame Snow! It was you who saved Persis and the baby, as she has often told me. Poor Madame Snow, she is dying of distaste. I have persuaded her master to sell her in Quebec."

At the word "sell" Seth spoke without taking time to think.

"Sell Mrs. Snow like a black to work in the kitchen?" he cried angrily, his heart beating at the idea that they could all be bought and sold like so many Guinea slaves. He had thought of himself as a captive, completely in Bedagi's power, but to be sold for money to white people seemed more degrading.

Father de la Pré flushed painfully, looked at him, and dropped his eyes.

"She would be kindly treated," he stammered, "and clean. It is the dirt she cannot bear."

Seth had had more time to think.

"You are right, Father," he said, "even I can see that she will die here."

He had a glimpse of Tarumkin who scowled at him without speaking, and toward evening, as he was fetching wood, he saw John Hammond coming toward him. He could never be mistaken in those huge shoulders and the small head with its cocky pose. For a moment he had a strange illusion that half of John Hammond's face was blackened, but it was only the shadow—when he turned, his whole face shone copper gold in the sunset.

Seth flung himself upon him and felt his ribs almost crack beneath the big man's bear hug.

"Well, it is good to see you," said John Hammond. "I'm glad I waited a few days more." He lowered his voice and glanced arrogantly but carefully about him before going on. "Some day soon I mean to try to escape. Will you come with me, Seth?"

XX

BOUGHT

ONE morning early Persis burst into Bedagi's house.

"We're going to Quebec! We're going to Quebec today!" she cried to Seth. Then she fearlessly knelt beside the seated Bedagi, twining her arms about his neck.

"Mrs. Job says John Hammond may come. Please, uncle, let Seth come with us, too," she coaxed.

Bedagi had just sold his skins to the trader at a good price and was feeling well disposed.

"Go, then, my son," he said to Seth. "You will see a great city. There are many of your nation there, too, working for the French. But remember that the soldiers send back to St. Francis any of our slaves who try to hide there, and then—" He grinned. "You come home like a good boy," he added.

Seth nodded. No, he would not try to escape, not even with John Hammond. The assurance lay strongly within him that some day he would reach home. He dared not risk that return on any foolhardy action, and he could not ignore his dream, at which John Hammond only laughed.

But this bright morning, all care dropped from him.

With Natanis they went to Quebec in one canoe. Mrs. Snow was tense with excitement. She had no feeling of disgrace in being sold, to her it was like being redeemed—anything so that she might get away from the Indians and get Persis away from them. Her only fear was lest no one might want them.

It seemed strange to Seth to be walking on cobbled streets between stone buildings from whose high peaked roofs little windows glistened in rows. All the people seemed so well dressed.

"My mother looks as fine as you," he murmured to himself as a lady passed them with her maid on the way to market, "—on the Sabbath, anyway," he added truthfully. Or, again, "My father is as handsome a gentleman as any of you," he thought as the Frenchmen went by, glancing carelessly at the English boy in the frilled shirt and stained Indian leggings and breechclout.

There were squares and churches, the sound of feet on cobbles, and the ringing of bells. Natanis was not experienced in selling a captive in Quebec. After knocking at many doors and meeting blank faces, they were finally taken into a kitchen in the upper town by a serving boy; and later two ladies, dressed with an elegance Seth had never seen before, entered and began looking at Mrs. Snow, talking her over together in their quick French tongue.

Mrs. Snow smiled at them and curtseyed as well as she could in her Indian dress. Excitement had brought a faint rose to her cheeks.

"Tell them that I am strong, strong," she said to Natanis. "I will work for them from dawn until dark. Tell them that I eat very little."

When he had spoken in his halting French, the lady in blue looked at Mrs. Snow with real pity.

"I would take her, for the English have a good reputation as servants," she told the Indian, "but I do not want a child in the house."

Persis ran to the other lady, who was dressed in black, and catching her hand, looked trustingly into her face.

"Don't send Mama back to St. Francis," she said, "please don't send her back. She loves clean things so."

The lady in black patted Persis on the head and dabbled at her eyes with a small lacy handkerchief. In a very sad voice she spoke to the lady in blue, who nodded and after a little more talk with Natanis drew out a purse and counted silver into his hand. The lady in black did the same.

"The black lady is the blue lady's friend. She does not live here," he explained to the four English people. "Her own little girl has died and in memory of her she buys Persis and will pay for sending her to the holy Ursulines. We are to take her to the convent, and on our way home you others may stop to say goodbye to your friend."

Mrs. Snow wept a little at the parting.

"But you will be away from the savages, Persis. I will think of you as lying in a bed, and eating clean food. Do not forget your catechism, my child," she said, trying to smile at the little girl who smiled bravely back, scarcely understanding what was happening in the excitement of so many new sights and sounds and experiences.

But in the cold stone parlor of the Ursulines Persis suddenly lost heart and clung to Seth.

"Don't let them take me, Seth. Don't let them take me!" she cried, burying her face in his frilled shirt and wetting it with the quick flood of her tears.

The nun behind the little grille spoke to her in English.

"There is a fawn in our garden," she said, "among the roses. It has a silver collar," and slowly Persis heard her through her sobs. "Your mother will come to see you and then you may show her the fawn. Say goodbye to your friends quickly, and I will take you to see it."

With a hasty kiss to all three, including Natanis, Persis was gone, but when they reached the street Seth's frilled shirt was still wet where she had cried.

He asked Natanis about the nun. Ah, yes, she was English, the Indian answered without surprise. There were many English among the Ursulines. The little captive girls were sent to the convent, perhaps as Persis had been sent, and some were redeemed and some married Frenchmen and some became nuns. They were very holy women, the Ursulines.

Natanis was in a hurry; his pouch was heavy with silver and he was anxious to be off. Perhaps he did not wish to be alone with the two Englishmen on the river after dark. But since her house lay on their way to the landing, he allowed them a minute in which to say goodbye to Mrs. Snow. When they knocked at the door, it was she who opened it, but they would scarcely have recognized her in her French clothes and heeled shoes, with a white starched cap on her hair. Her face shone with hot water and soap; already she moved more vigorously.

"Madame is very kind," she told them, "and oh, everything is so clean, so clean!"

Then she asked about Persis, clapping her hands softly like a girl when they told her she might see her child.

"I am so happy!" she said. Then her face clouded and a deep tender sadness came into her eyes. "But I do not wish to say goodbye to you."

It was at John Hammond she was looking.

Natanis called to them impatiently from the street. It was time to go.

"God bless you," said Mrs. Snow in the doorway, her voice trembling.

"God bless you and keep you," said John Hammond, and only Seth heard him add under his breath, "my dearest dear."

XXI

John Hammond Runs Away

LIFE at St. Francis was pleasant in the summer. As
Keoka had told him, they lived here mostly in bark
houses, two or three families to a house, and there was
less smoke and a little more room. The village was
palisaded with four gates that were closed at night, for
the Mohawks had been known to attack the Algon-
quin and Huron towns even under the cannon of the
forts at Quebec, so greedy were they for killing. What
Seth liked especially about St. Francis was the falls

whose sound might be heard day and night, mingled with all the sounds of Indian life, swelling and dying away and swelling again, beating always against his ears like the heart of the earth throbbing and throbbing. The Indians kept their canoes both above and below the falls, some to go up the Chaudière for hunting or fishing and the larger fleet for the mouth of the river, and the St. Lawrence, and Quebec, not ten miles away.

Outside the south gate, at a little distance, stood the Jesuit mission church and the priest's house where Father de la Pré and his French serving man lived. Along the river, too, lay the cleared land for corn and beans and squash. It was early summer now and safe to plant the corn, even in this cool air. The women all worked together putting the seed in the hills which they scraped into shape with short-handled hoes, chatting and laughing as they bent over their tasks. Seth attempted John Hammond's rebellion of the first fall, when put to work with the squaws, but only got a good thrashing from Bedagi for his pains, at which all the women laughed except Keoka. She often worked beside him, and although now he knew the Indian words for everything, he still taught her English, and she talked to him in polite stiff little phrases in their own language. On Sundays he went to mass with all the village, but he and most of the other captives stood near the door and only bowed their heads when the rest knelt. He had liked Father Simon from the first, but Father de la Pré's stumbling speech and averted eyes filled him with a kind of pity and contempt.

"He is a woman," he said to Bedagi one day, as they watched the young priest walking from the church with his uncertain step, his eyes on the ground, his lips smiling uneasily.

But Bedagi said emphatically, "You are a fool, judging the corn only by the husk."

Cold and famine were things forgotten now; rain was nothing to Seth any more; he knew the sky by day and by night as he knew his right and his left hands. Long ago the giant of the winter had wheeled for a last time below the horizon and now he learned the Indian names for the summer stars. He could tell the wind from the shape of the clouds and foretell storm by mosses and fur. With the other boys he speared fish in the pools of the streams that fed into the Chaudière, and hunted with them with bows and arrows, and in the evening gambled with peachstones. He had never been adopted, but Bedagi and his wife treated him like any of their children. The work was light, the hours of play were long and carefree, except for his fear for John Hammond's safety.

The big man, he knew, was storing supplies of jerked

meat and cornmeal, a very little at a time. He was an excellent hunter and was allowed the use of a gun, but his bullets were counted and his powder weighed out to him, and he was forced to account for every shot. Nevertheless, Seth knew that he cut the bullets in two and used the powder in light charges and already had a good supply of powder and shot hidden away in a certain dry cave he had discovered. It was now only a matter of time before John Hammond would leave. Each night, Seth dreamed of his half-blackened face and woke in the morning with a sense of apprehension and despair, for it was as natural to Seth to feel deeply for other people as it was to think in a series of clear-cut pictures.

More than once he begged John Hammond to wait.

"A commission will come," he would urge. "Don't go! You know what it means to be caught, and Tarumkin is always sneaking about, watching for a chance to make trouble."

But John Hammond would not wait.

"Now that Mrs. Job is safely married and Mrs. Snow is in Quebec, I have nothing to keep me, boy," he said. "I must go back and see how my bad-tempered old father is. And I'll take them all your respects."

One evening as Seth was sitting by the fire with Bedagi and his family, making a toy for the youngest

child, he heard voices outside and in a moment Tarumkin lifted the elkskin at the door and stepped quickly
into the room, looking eagerly about with his squinting eyes.

"Is Long Chief here?" he demanded, and Seth felt
his heart sink. The moment had come.

"He will be back soon," he tried to say calmly. "He
has lost his way or his canoe has sprung a leak."

If John Hammond were gone, every minute gained
might help him.

But Tarumkin gave him a triumphant leer.

"We will light his way back," he said and turned
and was gone.

Outside, Seth could hear a gathering of people,
voices raised, and the barking of dogs.

"Ha," said Bedagi, expressionlessly, "young men go
hunting."

Seth, against his will, went with dragging feet to the
door to watch the war party go by.

The faint light of a waning moon shone along their
bodies and glinted in their eyes and on the heads of
the tomahawks in their belts and along the barrels of
the guns resting in the hollows of their left arms. When
they were gone, he looked up at the sky until a degree
of calm had come to him.

But John Hammond was not caught that night.

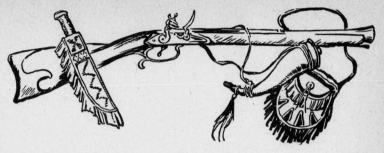

XXII

THE ORDEAL OF HOPE

VERY early the next morning the young men left again to continue their search for John Hammond. And this time they had with them provisions to last them for days without any need for hunting. Seth heard them go by and again a snakelike fascination drew him to the door of the house to see them pass, moving darkly in a dark world, though the first few bars of pink lay in the eastern sky below the serenity of the morning star.

A dog lapped his hand with a warm wet tongue, a man spoke, he saw the outlines of eagle feathers twisted in the scalp locks of the young men, where their heads and shoulders were outlined against the paler sky over the cornfields, and then they were gone.

All day long Seth's thoughts were with John Hammond; he, too, seemed to have run far, using all his cunning to blot out the trail; he, too, seemed to be lying hid while they searched for him. At every sound, Seth started up, his heart pounding, and he did his work with dragging steps, fumbling and forgetting, but both Bedagi and his squaw were kind to him.

That night he lay long watching the stars through the smoke vent, and when at last he fell asleep he again dreamed of John Hammond, still with his face blackened on one side, and woke with a dry throat and sobs racking his chest.

The next day the strain was increased, for now there entered into it the terrible ordeal of hope. There had been men who had escaped from the Indians and with every hour of security John Hammond's chances increased as the arc of his possible position swung wider and wider from the village. This second day Seth kept feverishly walking about, wandering up and down the river beyond the palisades. It seemed to him that he had never known the mosquitoes to bite so, and the July sun beat down on the ripples of the Chaudière in blinding stabs of light, and the sound of the waterfall, which he usually loved, now throbbed in his ears with a maddening insistence.

In the late morning a little breeze came up which

helped with the mosquitoes and brought a distant sound
of bells and cannon from the direction of Quebec.
Keoka joined him quietly.

"The first ship from France has come," she said,
scarcely above a whisper. "They always ring the bells.
It brings the news of the world, all that has happened
since November. Perhaps peace has been declared,
Seth. Perhaps the old king is dead."

Seth looked at her and saw that though her voice was
steady her eyes were red from crying.

"Will they bring him back, Keoka?" he asked her.

"I don't know," she said with a shiver. "Once two
men escaped."

And Seth saw that she had little hope.

Again a flaw in the wind stirred the leaves and
brought with it the sound of the far-off church bells
and the dull roar of cannon and a confusion that might
have been the cheering of men's voices. All the city's
two thousand would be down on the quays; for a moment his mind imaged those sails slowly taking shape
above the horizon that had been bare of any sail all
winter and all the long spring and the early summer;
he saw the vessel against the Isle of Sorcerers with
sailors in the rigging, and priests and merchants, *voyageurs* and traders, market women with their dogcarts

123

beside them, ragged boys and the soldiers in their gay uniforms, and even the old governor, the Count de Frontenac, from his Château St. Louis above the city, waiting to shake hands with the captain and ask the news of Europe.

"Peace may have been made months ago, and no one here would know," Seth thought. "If there has been a treaty, the commission will come to redeem us."

But it would be too late to redeem John Hammond.

Keoka gave his hand a quick warm grasp, looking up into his face.

"He *may* escape, Seth," she said, and seeing that he was too miserable to answer her, she slipped quietly away.

It was the beginning of the eel-fishing season, and the racks down on the shingle were covered by drying eels, where the flies gathered. Through the willows the continual motion of falling water held Seth's hopeless eyes. The sound came in a series of rhythms and beats joining into greater rhythms, and just as his ear felt it had solved the skein of sound, the rhythm escaped again, and his ear was confused in seeking the law underlying it, as his eye was in watching the surges and breaking arrow tips of spray.

A man was singing somewhere out of sight beyond the willows, a love song Seth had often heard.

THE ORDEAL OF HOPE

*"There we will sit, on the beautiful mountain,
    and listen to the Thunder beating his
    drum.*
*We will see the flashes from the lit pipe of
    the Lightning.*
*We will see the great Whirlwind race with
    Squall.*
There we will sit until all creatures drowse."

As the sun rose in the sky and the heat increased,
the boy found himself weak with hunger, but the
idea of returning to Bedagi's house and the smarting
reek of smoke, and eating gobbets of meat in that
throng of scratching dogs and crowding children,
while he tried to hide his misery from Bedagi's eyes,
seemed worse than hunger. Almost unconsciously, his
feet followed the path that brought him beyond to the
church and the priest's little house.

Martin la Tour, the priest's servant, was weeding in
the garden among the young cabbages, and beyond there
were turnips and peas and a little field of barley. Near
the house stood some young apple and pear trees, and
the priest's cow was staked out in the meadow. As Seth
watched her, she lay down; for a moment her calm
beauty was lost in a series of awkward movements and
then regained as she lay serenely chewing her cud,

her tail switching the flies. All these things that were like the things at home reassured Seth's torn feelings, and when Martin straightened his back to give him a friendly good morning, he answered with more hope than he had felt for many hours.

"You would like to see the good Father, my friend?" asked Martin.

"Oh, no," said Seth quickly. "I would not trouble him."

"It does not trouble him," said Martin going into the house.

And in some way Seth found himself eating a salad off a china dish and rolls fresh from the oven, and drinking hot chocolate with the priest in his small bare study with the maps and crucifixes on the wall.

But Father de la Pré, himself, was as ill at ease in his own house as ever, hesitating for words when he spoke and looking at anything but Seth. The boy was relieved after the repast when the Jesuit said that he must return to a letter he was writing to his superior and suggested that Seth might like to work for a little with Martin in the garden. Stooping once more close to the earth, with the sun hot on his back and his fingers brown with soil and weed stains, the boy might have thought himself beside his father, helping him bring order out of the disordered wilderness. And Martin said little to him, save a friendly word now and then as their work brought them close together, but Seth could hear him whistling *"À la claire fontaine"* to himself.

The sun moved nearer the horizon, and the air grew cooler. There was a small day moon in the sky. Martin gave Seth a milking stool and a pail and he went out to the cow who lurched to her feet at his coming and stood breathing gently at seeing a stranger approach. But she allowed him to take his place at her left side, and soon the milk was drumming warmly into the pail. The priest's tabby cat appeared, mewing silently and looking up into Seth's face. Dexterously he squirted a thin jet of milk toward her, which she expertly caught in her open mouth as he expected. How often the Snows' cat had come to him at milking time, and sat afterwards, as this one did, cleaning her whiskers with a careful paw!

It was almost dark when at last Seth, having been given a great bowl of bread and milk, made his way back toward the village. He might be punished for being away so long, but he thought no one would take any notice of it. The evening star trembled like luminous dew on the pale green of the sky.

The young men had been gone for two days now. Surely John Hammond had escaped! And then, as a sense of peace came to Seth such as he had felt on that August morning of the year before, he heard a cry rise from the darkness of the forest and hang triumphant and sinister in the quiet air, followed by another and another until the evening was shaken by the inhuman hootings that announced the return of a war party with a captive.

XXIII

Nightmare

THE entire village swarmed out of their gates with laughter and screamings to greet the return of John Hammond. Thrust here and there, buffeted, with sand thrown in his face, he walked with unmoved dignity, his small head at as defiant a set on his great shoulders as ever. He was naked, except for a breechclout, and had been painted black all over with powder and bear's grease. Seeing Seth, he made a motion of his head, and now the boy knew that the gesture in his nightmare had been one of both greeting and farewell. Everything was as he had dreamed it, except that John Hammond's face was now completely blackened.

Mrs. Job pressed against the captive, holding a bowl to his lips, and he took a long drink and thanked her before Tarumkin struck her out of the way. She was crying quietly as she stood for a moment beside Seth.

"I had no rum for Long Chief," she said, "but I gave him maple sugar and water to strengthen his courage."

"You are good," said Seth. "What will they do to him now?"

"They will burn him tonight," she answered, weeping. They were soon separated by the crowd, and Seth looked in vain among the dim twilight faces of the howling savages about him for one look of pity. But John Hammond had still another friend, after all, in the crowd.

A hand tugged fiercely at Seth's blanket and Keoka's voice hissed in his ear in English,

"What are you doing here? Get out of the crowd into the shadow. Don't let anyone notice you. And run for the priest as though wolves were after you. I will delay them here, if I can."

The shock of her voice filled with anger and desperation, and the touch of her ice-cold hand woke Seth from the trance of horror he had been in since he had heard the first hoot quivering under the evening star. The nightmare dissolved into dreadful reality.

"The priest can do nothing," he said.

"There is no other chance," she whispered back. "Run!" And she was gone.

Now Seth edged his way to the outskirts of the crowd, and drifted quietly out of sight between two cabins. Keeping the buildings between him and the Indians, he made south toward the priest's house. Once out of sight, he began to run. By now, the earth was almost pitch dark, and the fireflies were weaving their patterned dancing in the lowlands. Seth was running at his utmost speed, but he never stumbled : his feet seemed to follow the trail by some secret wisdom of their own, avoiding the stones, and in a few minutes he had burst open the door of the Jesuit's house and stood panting before Father de la Pré, pouring out his story while the young priest nervously fingered the crucifix at his breast, drumming with an uncertain hand on the table.

Having heard the boy's story, still without saying anything, the Father rose and taking the great key of the church from its nail on the wall—it was nearly a foot long—he followed Seth out into the darkness. But instead of turning toward the Indian town, he turned away toward the church. Seth heard the key rasping in the lock and the creak of the unwilling door. Not know-

131

ing what else to do, he followed the Jesuit into the damp darkness of the church, which smelled of old incense.

A light was burning in the hanging lamp before the altar, like a small red eye in the night about it, and dimly Seth saw Father de la Pré kneeling with bowed head. He, too, flung himself on his knees near the door, murmuring broken prayers, but under his closed eyelids frightful pictures kept forming. He started up to his feet and running forward touched the other on his shoulder.

The priest's face was like that of a drowned man turned up to him out of the black waters of darkness.

"I can do nothing," he said. Seth could have screamed. "Only God can do it through me," he added in a sort of whisper, and returned to his prayers.

A century seemed to pass before he rose to his feet, and followed Seth from the church, leaving the door wide open behind him.

"Run, my son," he said, "the time is short."

And fast as Seth ran, he heard the priest close behind him.

In the center of the village a stake had been planted in the ground and piled with branches. The Indians made a wide circle about it so that all might see, and within this ring some of the young men were dancing, and a few boys and young squaws were busy with tending the fire, which in some places was beginning to burn but in front seemed slow to catch, sending up instead wreaths of smoke that almost hid the figure of John Hammond painted with the black of death, his hands bound above his head.

Father de la Pré passed Seth and pushed his way into the open space.

"My children!" he cried in a loud deep voice from which all hint of uncertainty had passed. "Put an end to this accursed frolic! Does not the tame fawn return to the forest, and the snared bird, breaking its string, fly again to its nest in the tree? Is it not nature that the captive should seek to regain his own dwelling? I say that your great father, the governor, will redeem this man. Unbind him, then, in the name of God!"

He stopped, one hand raised, his eyes facing boldly into the hostile ring of faces. But no one moved to unbind John Hammond. The only sound was the small hiss and crackle of the young flames. Someone, perhaps Tarumkin, laughed derisively.

"This man has eaten and drunk with you, sat by your side and hunted in your parties. You have greatly praised his strength and skill. Once more I say turn not against him as wolves turn, my children! Once more I say, unbind him!"

But no one stirred and the smoke wreaths almost hid John Hammond from sight.

Then a change came over the face of Father de la Pré. It seemed glazed with a sort of madness, and his voice rose—high and menacing,

"Ah, children of the devil!" he cried. "Why should I try to save you from your own acts, I who hold the keys of heaven and hell! You defy me, you filthy spawn of Satan, and I shall thrust you down into the depths where the fires burn forever, tended by Mohawks, guarded by Iroquois! There you shall prove if you be men, under the knives and in the torture fires, until the moon rises no more in the sky and the sun shines no longer on the earth. See, with this key," and from his breast he drew the great key of the church and brandished it above their heads, "I open the doors of hell wide for you, and the hands of the Iroquois devils reach out to seize you by the hair!"

But the crowd was weeping and kneeling, rocking back and forth. "Father, have pity! Father, we obey you!" they moaned, and men and women jostled each other to untie John Hammond and lift him down from the stake, while others beat out the fires.

The Jesuit stood, icy and inhuman, in his place, beckoning to this Indian and that.

"I shall need you and you and you," he said, "to take

me with this man to Quebec tonight. Haste! Haste! I hear the flames that are never extinguished leaping up to receive you! Even now I hesitate to balk them, you who are naturally as evil as serpents!

"Keep where you are, you others!" he cried harshly, as Tarumkin moved forward. "Let no man whom I have not pointed out follow me, lest I close upon him the gates of darkness!"

They were gone—a strange procession, John Hammond with a blanket thrown about him, followed by the priest, with the three Indians cowering at his heels. No one stirred, but the waterfall sounded loudly through the night. Then Seth made out on the river the deeper darkness of a canoe moving rapidly away. Keoka's voice startled him.

"They went just in time," she said very low. "Oh, I thought you were never coming! I helped bring the boughs and managed to wet the ones nearest Long Chief, but I thought you would not come in time!"

And Keoka, who had not cried in danger, cried now with relief as though her heart would break.

XXIV

Ensign Finds His Master

BEDAGI and his brother were restless. It was not their custom to stay long in any village, like the Hurons, and the terrible Five Nations. They followed the migrations of the animals, and as they found game scarce about St. Francis, and soon wearied of eel fishing, they were anxious to leave on a hunting trip. Besides, they wished to have new furs to trade for tobacco when the Tobacco Nation should come down the river in their great fleet of trading canoes about the time of the corn harvest. The Tobacco Nation grew most of the tobacco and the Hurons most of the corn which was traded; the Montagnards sent their canoe fleets up the river with sealskins, seal oil, and whale oil, too, and the Indians at the mission villages had dried eels and furs. Harvest time was a time of feasts and meetings and inter-tribal trade and Bedagi wished to be ready for it.

Seth was not sorry to leave St. Francis for a while. He knew that John Hammond was safe in a Quebec prison; even Mrs. Snow and Persis he had seen only once, and Persis, with the quick forgetfulness of little children, had screamed at sight of him and called him an Indian. It had taken all his skill and the little birch basket full of blueberries which he had brought with him to coax her to his knee; but once perched there, she had suddenly taken his head between her hands and kissed him, which had pleased him greatly. But soon a pleasant-faced nun had come for her, since it was time for her sewing lesson, and he had once more found himself in his old Indian clothes, a stranger amid all the French bustle of the city.

At St. Francis he made no new friends; talk with Father de la Pré was as difficult as it had been before that shattering night, and though he sometimes worked beside Martin for a few hours, it was with Keoka that he spent most of his time.

They were only to be gone until the corn was ripe and though he missed the girl at first, he was soon caught up in the life on the river. The St. Lawrence was the highway of Canada, for a thousand miles of wilderness holding together the scattered towns and forts, the farms and the friendly tribes. Up and down it came the boats in summer and the dogsleds in winter. They met many other small parties of Indians, but the great fleets of decorated birch-bark canoes would not be seen at this time of the year. Sometimes a French factor went by from one of the trading stations, or a couple of French or Indian *voyageurs* with bright caps, bringing a laden bateau up toward the city. On the second day, they waved to the sailors on *La Justice,* a French vessel coming up the river from France with new soldiers for the garrison and two or three young Jesuit priests, gazing out at this unknown world to which they had dedicated themselves. Their canoes were so close that Seth and his companions could make out the elaborate frogging on the coats of the soldiers and the small black books of devotion the "black gowns" held in their hands.

At Tadousac they stopped to see the whale fisheries and then turned their canoes back into the deep waters of the Saguenay between its buttresses of stone. Nothing in Seth's experience or the talk of the Indians had prepared him for this river. All his life he would remember the solemnity of the sunsets when the mountains that seemed shutting them in turned a transparent blue against the gold wings of the clouds and faded away to massive luminous outlines, at last only seen since they blotted out the stars and the pale flare of the northern lights.

Under those headlands, where the birches and evergreens grew from fissures in the headlong rock, their trunks parallel to the cliff to which they clung, there were few beaches, and often they traveled late from one camping place to another. It was on such an evening when the sky was molten copper in the west, and the dull water only caught the light in the ripples about a leaping fish, that Seth saw a fountain suddenly rise far ahead of them, rosy against the misty blue of the headlands.

"A whale!" he cried to Bedagi and once more, after a pause, rose the beautiful column of spray against the darkness, this time nearer.

Bedagi grunted out an order and the two canoes hugged the shore until the monster of the ocean had passed slowly by with a wake that made their light vessels rock. Seth always remembered that, too, as the night when there had been so many falling stars.

When the corn was ripe they returned to St. Francis, with a fair number of furs which were not as good as they would be in the winter. They had, however, several silver fox skins, and what was more valuable, a black fox, as well, so that the hunters were satisfied.

Now the harvesting was done, and the feasting and trading; the northern lights came brighter and bolder with every night, so that the sorcerers prophesied a cold winter; the rains came and the last mosquitoes died; the geese flew over, and the ducks and the little wood pigeons darkened the sun. All the pageant of the fall swept by them and the sumacs drooped their scarlet leaves like the feathers of war bonnets. Everything was once more dry and brilliant, and there was a continual rustling sound among the branches.

"It is the Winter," said Bedagi. "There is Winter and Spring," he told Seth. "They exchange dwellings, and when they are newly come, one may hear their speech, but no man is wise enough to understand it."

The moon rose slow and golden in the autumn skies.

"Why is she sometimes dark?" asked Seth and Bedagi told him, "Because she holds her son whose father is the Sun in her arms."

"Has she arms?" asked Seth.

"Assuredly, stupid one!" said Bedagi. "But she, like the Sun, always holds her bow straight before her, so no man sees her arms."

"And what does she hunt?" asked Seth.

"Who knows?" said Bedagi.

This year, they did not leave the village with the coming of the geese as they had done the preceding fall. The harvest and trading had both been good. They stayed and enjoyed their fleeting wealth, and the leaves fell and witch-hazel bloomed spidery yellow in the naked woods, and the snows came and the river froze.

And now all travel was by dogsled and snowshoe and it was the sky that was dark against a gleaming world, instead of itself being something that shone over an earth clad in the soft darkness of green. Christmas came and then New Year's and Father de la Pré gave Seth a coat for a New Year's gift, and Keoka a dress of red cloth sent from France for the Indians. Now it was almost time for Bedagi to be off, but although Seth did not greatly dread the winter in the wilderness, he tried to delay the setting out from day to day on one pretext or another. He, himself, could not have explained the impulse that moved him so strongly.

But the day before they were to leave, as he was bending over a pack he was preparing for the next day's trip, he heard the crunch of two pairs of feet and the sound of a Frenchman's voice, and a shadow fell across him. He had learned an Indian concentration and as he was busy he did not look up and the men moved away. But a few seconds later something hit him in the chest with great force and bowled him over in the snow amid a storm of lappings and joyous barkings. It was Ensign, who had recognized Seth and was almost beside himself with delight.

XXV

HER WEIGHT IN SILVER

WITH his father's arms close about him, and Ensign leaping against his knees and frantically licking his hands, Seth knew why he had delayed Bedagi's setting out. He heard the Frenchman slapping his thighs and laughing,

"Ha! Ha! We both thought you was Indian!"

But he scarcely noticed, with so many questions to ask his father about his mother and Abigail and Mrs. Snow's baby and the Hintons and all the rest at Pemaquoit. Even about John Hammond and the Snows, Mr. Hubbard had more to tell Seth than the boy could tell him, for he had seen them both in Quebec. John Hammond and Mrs. Snow had been married and the governor, pleased and touched by the romance, had promised them as a wedding present that they should be the first prisoners exchanged in the spring, and that Persis, who now spoke only French, should leave the nuns and go with them.

"Now there is only Keoka, sir!" said the boy, and he told his father of the English girl who had been brought up as an Indian and who had been kind to him since that first night when she led him from torture at the Penobscot village.

Mr. Hubbard looked troubled and shook his head doubtfully.

"I am afraid I have nothing more with which to redeem a captive," he said. "They put me off, Seth, time and time again, saying that a commission was soon to set out and that you would be exchanged for a French prisoner. When this summer went by, with still nothing done, I traveled to Boston and saw the governor who gave me a letter and a hundred pounds of Virginia snuff for the Count de Frontenac. I said to your mother, 'Ensign and I will go, if you are willing,' and she said, 'Go and God bless you.' We traveled alone, north through the wilderness, and reached here in twelve days, I on snowshoes, with Ensign pulling the snuff on the sled. The count arranged with Monsieur Dalbert, the interpreter, for redeeming you. They knew where you were likely to be found, because of a priest, Father Simon I think they called him, who had told him of how you and this girl aided him in the winter. Now, if only your master makes no trouble, this will be the happiest day in my life."

And Bedagi made no trouble. He took Mr. Hubbard's hand in his copper hand and said: "Me no let Indian adopt Seth. Keep him for you. Me know you come some day. In times back, you never cheat me. You let me lie by fire. Your woman feed me good. I take good care of your boy," and then he said to Seth, dropping the awkward English: "Our lodge will be empty without you, my son, but you will wish to return to those of your own blood. When the war is over some day, we shall come to see you again. Be happy in your life."

And he took the money that the Frenchman gave him without glancing at it, and put it in his pouch.

The other farewells were quickly taken. Father de la Pré had tears in his eyes as he blessed him, and Martin made him a gift of squirrel skins; Mrs. Job actually wept, as did all the household of Bedagi down to the youngest child, which howled against its mother's knee. But Seth had not given over the hope of redeeming Keoka. He had lived for two things: to return home and to take Keoka with him. His father was doubtful whether a girl could bear the hardships of such a trip, but Seth laughed at that.

"You do not know the life she has led, sir," he said.

145

"She has had to be the brave of their lodge and knows all there is to know of starvation and exhaustion. I think Natanis would take her grandmother, who is his aunt, under his care, but I do not know if she will let Keoka go, or if Keoka will go."

The girl was very quiet when they came to her cabin. She had already heard the news and cast a quick keen glance at Mr. Hubbard and the agent as she invited them into her grandmother's cabin. The old woman greeted them also suspiciously, but asked them to sit down, striking at the dogs to force them from the fire to make room for their guests. Before anything could be discussed, all must eat together, and Keoka, seeing Mr. Hubbard glance at his greasy wooden bowl flushed with shame. Snow had begun to fall and the place was full of acrid smoke that brought tears to the eyes and made everyone sit with head lowered as much as possible toward the clearer air near the earth.

Mr. Hubbard, least accustomed to the ordeal, began to cough stranglingly and Seth said: "Put your mouth to the ground, sir, and it will soon pass."

When the stew of venison and cornmeal had been eaten, Seth turned to the old woman and begged her to let Keoka go with them to her own people.

Her old face became full of doleful wrinkles.

"We are her own people," she cried. "I, myself, took

146

her and held her in the river, washing away from her every drop of her English blood. I clothed her in a little dress of doeskin, pretty with beadwork. I gave her the name of my dead granddaughter and made a feast of adoption. She is blood of my blood and bone of my bone. She has no desire to go with you."

"Is that true?" asked Seth.

Keoka was crying without sound.

"I love my grandmother," she said, "and an English house seems to me like a trap. Even the clothes of the English are a sort of trap, and so are their words and acts." She was silent for a moment and then she added in a sort of wail, "Still, my brother, I desire to go with you."

"You see, grandmother," cried Seth. "She wishes to go with us."

"I will sell her then," said the old woman sourly. "Give me her weight in silver and you shall have her."

XXVI

THE CLOCK

MONSIEUR DALBERT had disappeared from the room, but in a few moments he returned, his black eyes twinkling, and took his place once more by the fire.

"Ha!" he said, laughing. "Grandmother, what do you wish this ungrateful girl for? She is tired of you, and wishes to go with the lad. It is natural enough. Soon, in any event, you must make a wedding feast for her. I have something here far better that I brought for Bedagi, but did not need to give him after all."

"Her weight in silver," muttered the old woman obstinately, looking at no one.

"A girl," went on the Frenchman with his air of subdued amusement, "is nothing but a girl. This one, I have no doubt, is a good girl, but there are many like her. Now what I have here, no one in the village has, except maybe the priest, himself. It is a clock."

And he drew out a small very ornamental clock from under his coat and set it on the ground, where it stood ticking loudly.

There was silence, except for a soft flapping sound of flames and the scratching of a dog, rapping the bone of his hind leg against the hard ground. Amid all the fluctuating noises of St. Francis and the river and the wilderness that lay about it, the clock alone stood ticking its endless mechanical tick which never varied and never fluctuated.

"See, grandmother," went on Monsieur Dalbert's insinuating voice. "When it stretches its right hand to the earth, the sun rises. When its right hand points to the height of heaven, the sun stands there and declines as the finger declines until it is swallowed into the earth again. No one in the village has such a marvel."

By now the old woman was staring with her small bright eyes at the clock, and the others watched the struggle between the two, for as yet she had not spoken.

"Many will come to ask to see such a wonder," went on the Frenchman, "and they will bring you presents. There will always be meat in the kettle while the clock lives in your lodge. See, grandmother, you have heard its breathing, but you have not heard it speak. Now it will speak," and with an expert finger he twirled the hands a little and the clock beat eleven clear strokes.

"What does it say?" asked the old woman in spite of herself.

"It says, 'Put the kettle on, grandmother,'" said the Frenchman chuckling. "It has twelve speeches whose meaning I will teach you, and between speeches it says, 'I am here,' so that you will never be lonely." He paused a moment and then went on briskly, "Come, come! You must make up your mind. Do you wish to have the clock to bring you good luck, or shall I take it back with me where you will never hear its talk again?" And he made a motion as though to rise and put the clock back under his coat.

But now the old woman with trembling hands reached out for the treasure.

"As you say," she mumbled, "Keoka would soon be married. This will stay with me and talk to me until I die. You may have the girl, since she wishes to go."

"It is a bargain," said the Frenchman, taking her hand. "See, grandmother, I will show you what you must do to keep your clock in health."

Keoka kissed the old woman and wept.

"Natanis will surely take you into his lodge, grandmother," she cried, but the old woman scarcely heeded her, her eyes fixed on her new possession.

"The clock will take care of me, granddaughter," she said. "Hush, it is going to speak to me again. Oh, what a beautiful little voice, like a drum, it has! What does it say to me this time?"

But the Frenchman did not answer immediately.

"First, say goodbye to your granddaughter," he said, "and let the English go down to the dogsleds. Then, in peace, I will teach you all there is to know."

And so the old woman embraced Keoka, and they thanked each other for many years of kindness and love between them, and each cried a little; but the clock struck again, and the old squaw dried her eyes quickly, so as to see what her marvel was up to. Then Seth put his arm about Keoka and, at a gesture from his father, led her out of the Indian cabin that had been her home.

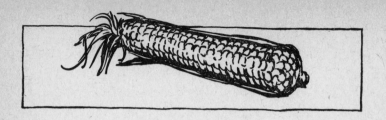

XXVII

The Red Ear

TWO weeks later, worn and almost snowblind, the three smelled salt air and came to a place where the woods ended at a rail fence and a white field smooth as a sea gull's wing sloped up to a square heavy-timbered house from whose wide chimney a little smoke was rising, with glimpses of deep blue winter sea beyond.

Ensign looked up at them with frantically wagging tail, waiting for help to take his sled through the fence; but Mr. Hubbard called him to heel while he unslung his powder horn, charged his gun, primed and fired it. A blue jay screamed angrily; a few gulls, wintering by the cove, flew up and circled over the roof, and after a moment the figure of a woman with a little girl behind her appeared about the corner of the house and stood shading her eyes to stare at them across the glare. Ensign gave a full-throated bark, and the woman began running toward them, struggling through the snow.

Then Seth swung over the fence, snowshoes and all, and ran up the slope as fast as his weary legs could carry him to catch his mother in his arms.

She brushed back her fair hair in the old way to look at him, laughing and crying: "Seth, you are a man now! Oh, to think that you are safe! God has answered my prayers. I think there has not been an hour since you left I have not prayed for you in my heart. And then when your father went into the wilderness after you, I sometimes feared that Abigail and I would be left all alone. Seth! Seth! Seth!"

And now Abigail, too, was crying, "Seth! Seth!" and it almost seemed that the sea gulls above were repeating the name, with their easy circling shadows sliding along the snow. And Zeke Hinton came to the door grinning, and Mrs. Hinton with two young ones, holding on to her skirts.

"That one's mine, Seth," she said as they entered the house, "and the other one is Mrs. Snow's. Is its mammy alive? And did the tawnies kill John Hammond?"

And so questions and answers crossed one another and the big room was filled with laughter and talk.

In all this, Keoka had no part. But Seth broke away and took her by the hand, telling his mother her story.

"I don't care who she is or where she comes from, if she was good to you, Seth. She shall be dear to me as one of my own children," said Mrs. Hubbard, taking Keoka in her arms.

Later in the day, she led the girl to her bedroom and when Keoka again stood in the doorway Seth scarcely recognized her—gone were doeskin and beaded bands, her silver armlets, and her soundless moccasins; instead, she stood like any English girl with her hair under a cap and wide skirts falling about her cobbler's shoes. Only her eyes were the same, looking at Seth with the patience of a captured wild thing, with a light creeping into them at his praise.

At her coming into the room, Seth's heart felt a deep flood of contentment, as though all he had cared for most in his two lives had been joined at last. He looked about him. The room was as he had so often pictured it to himself when he lay curled on the ground, sleepless with homesickness: the clean sanded floor, the stools and settle and table, the bright pewter, the smell of soap—they were all there as he remembered them, with his father standing on the hearth, and his mother at the spinning wheel with her fair hair straying from under her cap, and Abigail beside her; even Mrs. Hinton rocking the two big babies in the wooden cradle, and Mr. Hinton cleaning his gun at the settle, were a part of his memories, but touched with something natural and lovely by Keoka's presence.

He wandered to the window that looked toward the harbor and in a moment beckoned the girl to join him, which she did, moving silently in spite of her heavy shoes. For a little while they stood in silence together, leaning their foreheads against the cold pane, looking out at a white world where the white gulls circled against the sky and cast blue shadows on the snow. He began to point out things to her, in a low voice, to which the others paid no attention.

"You can't see well, now," he said, "but there is the inlet, and a fine beach for swimming. The fishing boats are along the shore, beyond the open water. Down there are the meadows, all cleared land, and this is where the English wheat grows right to the water's edge. Over there is the cornfield. You never saw such corn."

Keoka looked and then turned to Seth, "It is all as you used to tell me," she said in the same hushed voice. "This house is good, and its people are good. My heart understands that it is good to plant corn always in one's own field."

Seth caught his breath, but said nothing. He was thinking of a winter day by a frozen pond, far to the north, and of what they had said then, sitting beside the broken beaver's dam. It all seemed long ago, but here in his own house, looking across the snow-swept fields that he, himself, had helped to clear, he understood at last what before he had only felt. When he spoke again, it was in the Indian tongue.

"It is to me that you shall some day give the red ear of corn, Keoka," he said, "and I shall give you the leg of a deer," and they smiled at each other gravely and seriously, their faces dark against the white cold blaze of the snow and sunlight.

AUTHOR'S NOTE

THE first settlements in Maine were temporary fishing establishments made in connection with the drying grounds of the fishing fleets. Later, as the fur trade began to compete with the fisheries in profitableness, more permanent settlements were begun, and by 1665 the Royal Commissioners listed five small towns—Kittery, York, Wells, Scarborough, and Falmouth—as well as the plantations on the Kennebec, the Sheepscot, and the Pemaquid rivers. The land titles of Maine were at this period and for long afterwards very uncertain, because of overlapping English grants and unsettled disputes with the French as to boundaries. The country was savage and untamed, its wilderness extended into Canada, and its rivers were roads leading into the country of the enemy. The Indians indeed traded with the English fur traders to an extent which often caused serious concern in Quebec, but at bottom their interest lay with the French as against the English. In the first place the English were taking up their lands, driving away the game, and spoiling their fishing. They had only to look south to see to what desperate remedies the tribes of Massachusetts and Rhode Island had been driven by the white encroachments. In spite of certain exceptions, the English had no natural sympathy with the Indians. They came to supplant them, and both races felt it.

But to the French, whose short summers discouraged farming, whose colonial existence depended almost entirely on the fur trade, whose religious energy was justified only by converts, and whose numbers demanded strong allies to help defend their outposts, the friendly tribes were a vital necessity. To the French the Indians were important alive. To the English it was always fundamentally true that a good Indian was a dead Indian.

Into this powder keg of hate and resentment and uneasy truce again and again for eighty years the wars between France and England across the sea recurrently dropped their burning torches. In 1688 Louis XIV was at war with William and Mary, and for eleven years and more this far-away dispute was a pretext for frontier expeditions and attacks during which many captives were taken to Canada and either kept in the Indian villages or sold to the French. Some died on the way; some, especially among those taken in young childhood, adopted the language and customs of their captors and married into French or Indian families or entered the religious orders; some—and with these is our concern—were redeemed and returned to their families to tell their stories of terror, hardship, and adventure. These stories were often made into pamphlets and formed a literature eagerly read at the time and still moving and vivid to the modern reader.

The settlers of Maine were on the whole fortunate in having to deal with the Abenakis, or "the Ancestors" as they were called by the other tribes. They seem to have been naturally less bloodthirsty than many of the other Indian nations, and the ideas of Christianity brought by the French had long had their effect among them, although a number of them were still pagan. Pagan or Christian, many families had accepted the invitation of the French at Quebec to form villages near the St. Lawrence, far away from English encroachments; and here they planted their summer corn, often returning for a time to their old haunts along the Maine rivers, where their kin still lingered.

The settlers did not think of the Indians as Abenakis. To them they were simply "the tawnies" or "the savages" or they named them for their river or one of their towns. Their knowledge of Indian customs was fragmentary and unrelated. To them each experience was a new thing outlined on a horror of flame and butchery. From the moment of their captivity to that of their final release, those who returned were never certain what would happen next. And the astonishing thing in the old chronicles is the variety of their experiences, wherein they met with everything at the hands of their captors from blood-curdling inhumanity to a chivalrous tenderness. The pattern of the captivities is much the same, beginning usually with a surprise attack, following through unbelievable hardships to a more settled form of life with either the Indians or the French, and ending in a negotiated release or, more rarely, an escape. But within this pattern the figures of the actors stand out sharply individualized. No two captives, and no two captors, ever behaved in the least alike.